“It’s a game of cat and mouse, isn’t it? We try to find the evidence and he tries to make sure we don’t. When is he going to give it up?”

Cam shrugged and pulled her out of the chair. “When he’s tired of playing cat and mouse.”

“Or when I’m dead.”

“Don’t say that.” He placed his hands on her shoulders and massaged his thumbs into her skin.

“We both know the reason why he hasn’t taken his shot at me yet.”

“We do?” Cam ran his tongue over his dry teeth.

“It’s because you’re here, Cam. He knows I have some kind of badass bodyguard dogging me, and when you leave—” her shoulders tensed beneath his hands “—I’m a goner.”

“I’m not going anywhere.”

“Yet.” She tucked her head beneath his chin. “How many more days until you leave?”

“Shh.” He dropped his hands to her waist and pulled her body against his. “We have time. I’m gonna catch this guy, and when I do, he’ll pay—for everything.”

DELTA FORCE DEFENDER

CAROL ERICSON

Recycling programs for this product may not exist in your area.

ISBN-13: 978-1-335-63952-3

Delta Force Defender

This edition published by arrangement with Harlequin Books S.A.

For questions and comments about the quality of this book, please contact us at CustomerService@Harlequin.com.

Printed in U.S.A.

Carol Ericson is a bestselling, award-winning author of more than forty books. She has an eerie fascination for true-crime stories, a love of film noir and a weakness for reality TV, all of which fuel her imagination to create her own tales of murder, mayhem and mystery. To find out more about Carol and her current projects, please visit her website at www.carolericson.com, "where romance flirts with danger."

Books by Carol Ericson

Harlequin Intrigue

Red, White and Built: Pumped Up

Delta Force Defender

Red, White and Built

Locked, Loaded and SEALed
Alpha Bravo SEAL
Bullseye: SEAL
Point Blank SEAL
Secured by the SEAL
Bulletproof SEAL

Target: Timberline

Single Father Sheriff
Sudden Second Chance
Army Ranger Redemption
In the Arms of the Enemy

Brothers in Arms: Retribution

Under Fire
The Pregnancy Plot
Navy SEAL Spy
Secret Agent Santa

Harlequin Intrigue Noir

Toxic

Visit the Author Profile page at Harlequin.com.

CAST OF CHARACTERS

Martha Drake—A brainy CIA translator responsible for turning over the emails that first implicated Delta Force's Major Rex Denver in a terrorist plot. She's now having second thoughts about the veracity of those emails, but it might be too late. Now someone wants her to keep her mouth shut.

Cam Sutton—This impulsive Delta Force soldier will do anything to clear his commander's name, including confronting the CIA translator who first discovered the phony emails implicating him. He soon realizes the translator is on his side, and now he must do everything in his power to protect her.

Casey Jessup—Martha's roommate may seem like an airhead, but she may be more politically connected than Martha realizes. Those connections might not be enough to keep her out of danger.

Congressman Robert Wentworth—This politician winds up dead in Martha's town house, but his death can't be connected to the emails...can it?

Tony Battaglia—A bartender who knows too much for his own good, and doesn't know when to keep quiet.

Sebastian Forsythe—A fellow nerd, Sebastian and Martha dated a few times. He's good at fixing computers. Is he also good at planting evidence?

"Ben"—He seems to have his fingers in all the pies, but nobody can identify him and nobody knows his real name. He may be the key to absolving Major Denver or he may be the major's worst nightmare.

Major Rex Denver—Framed for working with a terrorist group, the Delta Force commander has gone AWOL and is on the run. He knows he's onto a larger plot, and he can count on his squad to have his back and help clear his name.

Prologue

A bug scuttled across his face, but Major Rex Denver didn't move one coiled, aching muscle. Twenty feet below him at the bottom of the hill, an army ranger team thrashed through the bushes, their voices loud and penetrating in the dead of the Afghan night.

Rex clenched his jaw as if willing the rangers to do the same. Didn't they realize this mountainous area was crawling with the enemy?

His eye twitched. To those rangers, Major Rex Denver *was* the enemy.

He didn't blame those boys for being out here searching for him. Hell, he'd be out here hunting down a traitor to his country, too.

He resettled his rifle and rested his finger on the trigger, not that he'd ever use it against any branch of the US Military. If the rangers found him, he'd go peacefully—but they'd never find him.

He'd started as a ranger himself, and after twenty years in Delta Force, leading his own team, he'd honed his skills at subterfuge and escape to perfection. They wouldn't catch him, but he'd die before he allowed the enemy that roamed these hills to catch those rangers.

One of the rangers yelled out. "Come out, come out, wherever you are."

Rex rolled his eyes. If that soldier was on his team, the wrath of hell would come down on him for that behavior. Rex had to bring the hammer down on Cam Sutton, one of the younger Delta team members, more than a few times for reckless behavior.

Someone issued a whispered reprimand from out of the darkness.

The young soldier answered back. "I don't care, sir, this is wrong. Major Denver's no traitor."

Rex believed he had the loyalty of most of the soldiers who knew his reputation, but the evidence against him was overwhelming. Why him? He and his Delta Force team must've stumbled on something big for someone to take them out of the picture. And he hoped to have a long time to figure it out.

A twig cracked to his right, and Rex's gaze darted toward the sound. Something glinted in the thick foliage. He flipped his night-vision goggles over his eyes and picked out the man crouched in the shadows, his focus on the team of rangers below.

Adrenaline flooded his body, and his heart hammered in his chest. Were there more? He scanned the area beyond the stealthy intruder. If this interloper wasn't solo, his companions weren't within striking distance of the rangers…at least not yet and not before the rangers could respond with their own firepower.

If Rex took out the enemy, he couldn't do it quietly. And once he made his position known, the rangers would swarm the mountainside and capture him.

He cranked his head around slowly, eyeing the steep drop-off behind him. He'd seen worse.

Rex popped up from his hiding place, and in the same motion he took the shot. It took just one. The enemy combatant pitched forward, his gun shooting impotently into the sky above him.

The rangers came to life as they fanned out and charged the hill.

Rex clutched his weapon to his chest, and rolled off the edge of the cliff into the dark unknown.

Chapter One

Martha's head pounded, and her hand trembled as she clicked open her email. Holding her breath, she scrolled past all the new emails that had come in since she'd taken lunch.

When she came to the end of the batch, she let out that breath and slumped in her chair.

The most sinister email that had come through was a reminder to submit her time sheet. She picked up her coffee cup and had to set it down as the steaming liquid sloshed over the rim onto her unsteady hand.

"Hey, Martha. Did you have a good lunch?"

Martha twisted her head around and smiled at her coworker Farah. "Errands, you?"

"Hot lunch date with the mystery man."

"I hope he's not married like the previous one."

"The previous one is still in the picture. A girl has to keep her options open." Farah winked and pushed away from Martha's cubicle almost bumping into Sebastian.

He held up his hand in an awkward wave. "Everything working okay with your computer after I dialed back that program to the previous version?"

"It's back up to speed. Thanks, Sebastian." Martha made a half turn in her chair back to her desktop, hoping he'd take the hint. They'd dated once or twice, but she wanted a relationship with some flying sparks for a change.

Sebastian took a step back, tapping the side of her cube. "Okay, then. Let me know if you need anything else."

Yeah, sparks.

Martha swung around to fully face her computer and jumped when another email came through. When would this fear go away? Those emails had started trickling into her inbox four months ago. She'd turned them over to the appropriate authorities and washed her hands of them—or tried to.

She chewed on her bottom lip. She hadn't forgotten about those emails. How could she, when they'd resulted in a huge investigation of some hotshot Delta Force commander, who'd then gone AWOL? How could she, when ever since she'd clicked on those emails, someone had been spying on her, following her?

She glanced over her shoulder at her coworkers in the CIA's translation department. Why had she been chosen for the honor of receiving those anonymous emails accusing Major Rex Denver of treason and colluding with the enemy?

What would've happened if she'd deleted those emails and never told a soul? Would she be the nervous wreck she was today?

She tapped her fingernail against her coffee cup. She couldn't have ignored those emails any more than she could jump up on her desk right now and scream in the middle of a CIA office that she had a bomb under her desk.

Maybe if she'd gotten rid of the emails like she was supposed to do, the people who'd sent them would leave her alone. But why would that matter? The senders had gotten their desired response. She reported the emails, which prompted the investigation of Denver, which then led to the discovery of his traitorous activities. The man had gone rogue. How much more guilty could you get?

But some gut instinct had compelled her to hang on to the emails. When she first received them, she'd copied them to a flash drive, which she wasn't even supposed to insert in her computer, and taken them home. She'd told everyone, including her slimy boss, Gage, that she'd deleted them. Then the IT department had come in and wiped her deleted items off the face of the earth.

She had her own suspicions about how those messages had gotten through to her email address at the Agency. It had the fingerprints of Dreadworm, a hacking group, all over it, but not even Dreadworm had claimed responsibility for forwarding those emails.

Martha had wanted to take a more careful look at the messages because of the phrasing. She spoke several languages, and she'd told Gage that the emails sounded like a foreigner had composed them.

He'd brushed her off like he always did, but she'd gotten her revenge by keeping those emails for herself.

Now she had someone stalking her.

Sighing, Martha straightened in her chair and shoved in her earbuds. She double-clicked on the file she'd been working on before lunch and began typing in the English words for the Russian ones that poured into her ears from one of the radio broadcasts the CIA monitored and recorded. After about an hour of translating, Martha plucked out the earbuds and stretched her arms over her head.

She swirled the coffee in the bottom of her cup and made a face. Then she slid open a desk drawer and grabbed a plastic bag with a toothbrush and toothpaste.

When she returned to her desk ten minutes later with a minty taste in her mouth and a bottle of water, she plopped in her chair and tucked her hair behind her ears, ready to tackle the remainder of the afternoon.

She glanced at the bottom of her computer screen, noticing a little yellow envelope on her email icon, indicating a new message. She double-clicked on it and froze. Her blood pounded in her ears as she stared at the skull and crossbones grinning at her from the computer screen, its teeth chattering.

Hunching forward, she resized the window and scrolled from the top to the bottom of it. No text accompanied the image. She scrutinized the unfamiliar email from a fake email account at the top of the window.

She glanced over her shoulder, and in a split second she forwarded the email to her home address. She deleted it and then wiped it clean from her deleted items. She knew it still existed somewhere in cyberspace, but not unless someone was looking for it. And why would anybody be checking her emails? She'd been the good little soldier she always was and turned over the others. The people up the chain of command had no reason to suspect her, and

Gage thought she was a lifeless drone, so she didn't need to worry about him.

If Gage cornered her right now and asked her why she didn't tell anyone about the skull and crossbones, she wouldn't have an answer for him. Maybe because she'd been dismissed so thoroughly after turning over the first batch. Not that this message had anything to do with the others—did it?

Of course it did. The same people had just sent her a warning, but she didn't know why. She didn't know anything about those emails or what they meant—but she was determined to find out.

The rest of the afternoon passed by from one jumpy incident to the next. Her scattered focus had been worthless in her attempts to translate the recorded broadcast.

Fifteen minutes away from quitting time, Farah hung on the corner of Martha's cubicle, her dark eyes shining. "I'm meeting my guy for a drink after work tonight. Do you want to come along?"

Martha crossed her arms. "And be a third wheel? No, thanks."

"He might have a friend." Farah made her voice go all singsongy on the last word as if to heighten the temptation.

"That's even worse than being a tagalong. A blind date?"

"Oh my God, Martha. Get used to it. It's the way of the world now."

"Seems to me all online dating has gotten you is a couple of sneaky married men."

Farah pouted. "It's fun. Not every date has to be a lifetime commitment."

"Go then and have fun for me." Martha waved her hand.

Not that she'd have accepted Farah's invitation under any circumstances, but after the day Martha had just had, she'd rather be home with a good book—and those emails.

She wrapped up her work and logged out of the computer, removing her access card and slipping it into her badge holder.

Waving to the security guard at the front desk, Martha pushed out the front doors and snuggled into her jacket. Winter in DC could be mild, but this November weather was already putting a chill in her bones.

She caught the next plain-wrap CIA van that shuttled employees from Langley to Rosslyn. When the van finally lurched to a stop, Martha stashed her book in her bag, rubbed her eyes and readjusted her glasses. She stepped out of the van and into the cold night, making her way to the Metro stop on the corner.

Descending into the bowels of the city with the rest of the worker bees, she welcomed the warmth from the pressing crowd as she turned the corner for her train. She jostled for position among the crush of people, gritting her teeth against the screech of the train's wheels slowing its progress.

As the lights approached from the tunnel, a man crowded her from behind. Martha tried to take a step back, but found herself pitching forward instead as someone's elbow drove into her back.

The train screeched once more, and Martha felt herself teetering on the edge of the platform. She thrust her arms in front of her as if to break a fall…but the only thing breaking this fall was that train barreling toward her.

Chapter Two

Cam curled his arm around the waist of the woman floundering on the precipice of the platform and pulled her back against his chest. He jerked his head to the side, but the man who had been crowding Martha Drake from behind had wormed his way through the crowd, the black beanie on his head lost in a sea of commuters.

Martha's back stiffened and she tried to turn in his arms, but he tightened his hold on her until the train came to a stop in front of them.

The doors whisked open, and Cam nudged her forward, whispering in her ear. "Go on."

She squeezed into the train with a mass of other people, grabbed a pole and spun around, her eyebrows snapping over her nose. "Take your hand off me."

Cam's jaw dropped open and a rush of heat claimed his chest. He'd just saved the woman's life, and this was the thanks he got?

He wrapped his fingers around the pole above her hand and twisted his lips. "You're welcome."

"I—I..." She shoved some wispy brown bangs out of her eyes, which blinked at him from behind a pair of glasses. "Yes, you're the one who pulled me back. Thank you. But..."

Lifting his eyebrows, he asked, "Yes?"

"How do I know you're not the one who was crowding me from behind in the first place?"

"I wasn't. That guy took off."

Martha's eyes, a lighter brown than her hair, widened and her Adam's apple bobbed in her delicate throat.

His statement had scared but not surprised her, and he dipped his head to study her face for his next question. "Any reason for somebody to push you into the path of an oncoming train?"

"No." She pressed her lips together. "It was crowded. Everyone was moving forward. I don't think that was an intentional push."

"It's always crowded. Commuters don't generally fall onto the tracks."

She shifted away from him, and the odor from the sweaty guy behind him immediately replaced the fresh scent that had clung to Martha, which had been the only thing making this tight squeeze bearable.

"Well, thank you." She tilted her chin up, along with her nose, and dismissed him.

Looked like she'd perfected the art of dismissing obnoxious men, but Cam had a date with Miss Prissy-pants here, even if she didn't know it.

He left her in peace for the remainder of the ride, although her sidelong glances at him didn't go unnoticed, and the knuckles of her hand gripping the pole had turned a decided shade of white. He'd planted a seed of suspicion in fertile ground.

When the train jerked to a stop, forward and then backward, Martha peeled her hand from the pole, hitched her bag higher on her shoulder and scooted out of the car, with a brief nod in Cam's direction.

He exited the train and followed Martha up the stairs and out into the night air, its frigidity no match for Ms. Drake's.

Three blocks down from the station, she stopped in front of a crowded Georgetown bar, clutching her bag to her chest, and turned to face him.

He sauntered toward her, then wedged his shoulder against the corner of the building, crossing his arms.

"Why are you following me? I'm going to

call the police." She waved her cell phone at him.

"We need to talk, Martha Drake."

She choked and pressed the phone to her heart. "Who are you? Are you the one who sent the skull and crossbones?"

Skull and crossbones? That was a new one. He filed it away for future reference.

He shrugged off the wall and straightened his spine. "I'm Sergeant Cam Sutton, US Army Delta Force, and you discovered some bogus emails that compromised my team leader, Major Rex Denver."

Martha's expressive face went through several gyrations, and then she settled on suspicion, which seemed to be one of her favorites. "How do I know you're telling the truth?"

He pulled his wallet from his pocket and slipped out his military ID. He held it out to her between two fingers.

She wasted no time snatching it from him and holding it close to her face, peering at it through her glasses. After perusing it for at least a minute, she handed it back to him. "Bogus emails?"

"Major Denver never did any of those things in those emails—" he jabbed the corner of his ID card in the general direction of her nose "—and if you hadn't turned them over to the

Agency, Denver wouldn't be in the trouble he is now."

"If I hadn't..." She stamped one booted foot. "What did you expect me to do with them?"

"We can't keep talking out here. Let's go inside." He jerked his thumb toward the bar.

Her gaze bounced to the large picture window of the bar over his shoulder and back to his face. The crowd inside must've reassured her because she dipped her head once.

Cam circled around Martha and opened the door, holding it wide for her to pass through. As she did, he got another whiff of her fresh scent, which seemed to cling to her.

DC office workers, unwinding at the end of the workweek, packed every inch of the horseshoe bar. They seemed more interested in socializing and watching the football game on the TVs over the bar than quiet conversation, leaving a few open tables toward the back of the room, near the restrooms.

Cam placed his hand on the small of Martha's back and steered her toward one of those tables. She'd twitched under his touch but didn't shrug him off. He'd take that as a good sign.

When he pulled out her chair, her eyes beneath her arched eyebrows jumped to his face, and she mumbled, "Thank you."

After he took his own seat across from her, he folded his arms and hunched over the table. “Why weren’t you surprised that somebody tried to push you onto the subway tracks?”

Her nostrils flared, and then she pursed her lips. “I told you. I thought it was an accident. I still think so.”

“Really?” He reached across the table so quickly she didn’t have time to pull back, and smoothed his thumb over the single line between her eyebrows. “Then why are you jumpier than a long-tailed cat in a roomful of rocking chairs.”

Martha’s mouth hung open, and Cam didn’t know if it was because he’d presumed to touch her petal-soft skin, or because he’d laid on a thick Southern accent. That slack jaw made most people look stupid, but Martha couldn’t look stupid if she tried. It made her look—adorable.

“Cat?” Her soft voice trailed off.

“You know—long tails, rocking chairs going back and forth.” He hit the table with his flat hand, and she jumped. “Nervous, jittery. Don’t deny it.”

A cocktail waitress dipped next to their table and tossed a couple of napkins in front of them. “What can I get you?”

Cam plucked a plastic drink menu from a

holder at the side of the table and tapped a picture of one of the featured bottles of beer. "I'll have a bottle of this."

"I can't just point at a picture." Martha snatched the menu from his hand and flipped it over, studied it for what seemed like ten minutes and then asked about twenty questions about the chardonnays. When she finally tucked the menu back in its holder, she said, "I'll have a glass of the house chardonnay."

When the waitress dived back into the crowd, Cam drummed his fingers on the table. He needed to start at the beginning with Martha. She clearly liked to take things in order.

He took a deep breath and started again. "Can you tell me about those emails? Where they came from? What they said, exactly, or close to it?"

"I should report you." She flicked her fingers at him. "What are you doing in DC? Why aren't you on duty?"

Cam narrowed his eyes. She didn't want to report him. Her voice had quavered, and she'd broken eye contact with him. If she'd turned those emails over so quickly, there shouldn't be anything stopping her from turning him over—but she didn't want to go there.

"I'm on leave. I'm not here on any official business, just my own." He crumpled the cocktail napkin in his fist. "Look, I know Major Rex Denver, and I know he's innocent of these charges."

"He went AWOL." She sniffed. "Running indicates guilt."

"Not always." He smoothed out the napkin and traced the creases with the tip of his finger. "Not if you think there's a conspiracy against you and you're going to be railroaded."

"A conspiracy?" Her eyes widened and seemed to sparkle in the low light from the candle on the table.

"Here you go." The waitress set down their drinks and spun away before Cam could tell her to close out the tab and that he didn't need a mug.

He watched Martha over the bottle, as he tipped the beer down his throat. Maybe this night would be longer than he expected.

"We think someone is framing Denver, and it started with those emails."

"We?"

"The Delta Force team that Major Denver commanded. We were all—" he put down the bottle harder than he'd planned "—dragged in for interrogation. Do you know what that's like? You're doing your job, doing the right thing, and *bam*. They're lookin' at you like you're vermin."

She nodded and took a big gulp from her wineglass. "I do know what that's like. I turned over those emails and all of a sudden, I'm suspect. They're checking out *my* communications, *my* files."

Cam's pulse ticked faster. That's why Martha was none too anxious to report him. They'd grilled her, too.

"Exactly." He touched the neck of his bottle to her glass and the pale liquid within shimmered and reflected in Martha's eyes. *Whiskey.* Her eyes were the color of whiskey. And right now he was a little drunk just looking into them.

Cam cleared his throat and rubbed his chin. "I don't trust them, any of them. All I know is Denver is not guilty of those crimes, and I'm gonna prove it."

Martha took another sip of wine from her half-empty glass, her cheeks flushed like a rose stain on porcelain. "I'll start at the beginning with the emails."

"Did the CIA determine where they came from?" He scooted forward in his seat.

"I didn't get all the details because why would they tell *me* anything? I'm just the one who discovered them and turned them over." She cupped her glass in her two hands and rolled it between her palms. "They were looking at Dreadworm though, you know that hacking group?"

He nodded, not wanting to interrupt her flow. This stuff had been bothering her for a while, and he just became her receptacle—a very willing one.

"But I don't know if they ever determined how my email inbox became the target, or at least they never told me. Dreadworm was just the messenger, anyway. The conduit for the message, if you will—and that message was that Major Rex Denver had been working with a terrorist group plotting against the United States."

Cam slammed his fist on the table, the tips of his ears burning.

Martha held up her index finger. "But I noticed something strange about those emails."

"Yeah, they were filled with lies."

"Well, I don't know about that, but it didn't seem as if the person who composed the emails was a native English speaker."

Cam blinked his eyes and took another swig of beer. "Go on."

"If it were a foreign entity who sent those messages, why? Why would they care to warn US Intelligence about an American serviceman?"

"Our allies would care."

"Why wouldn't our allies just use regular channels to communicate with our military or even the CIA? But an unfriendly entity might have every reason to plant those stories about Denver."

"You've been thinking about this."

"It's more than just the emails." Martha waved her hand at the passing waitress. "Another round, please."

Cam cocked his head and took in Martha's empty wineglass and flushed cheeks. She'd downed that pretty fast. Although even in low heels she stood taller than most men, she was as slim as a reed, and the booze seemed to have loosened her tongue and her attitude toward him. He'd take it.

"More than emails?" He wrapped both hands around his bottle.

She looked both ways in the crowded bar and hunched forward, wedging her chin in the palm of her hand. "I'm being followed."

"The guy on the subway platform."

"I don't know." She drew back from him... and her earlier pronouncement, and tucked a lock of silky hair behind her ear. "Nobody has ever made physical contact with me before. That push could've killed me."

The fear in her whiskey eyes plunged a

knife in his gut. "Maybe it was just a warning, maybe a coincidence after all."

"You don't believe that."

"How do you know you're being followed?"

"I can feel it, sense it."

He rolled his shoulders and thanked the waitress as she brought them their drinks. Maybe Martha was just paranoid. She'd been dwelling on those emails, and he didn't blame her. They'd started a firestorm.

"And then there's the skull and crossbones."

He coughed and his beer fizzed in his nose. "You mentioned that before. Someone put a skull and crossbones on the emails?"

"Not the original messages. Someone sent me an email, just this afternoon, with one of those animated gifs of a skull and crossbones—blinking eyes and chattering teeth." She took a gulp from her new wineglass, and Cam placed his hand over her icy cold one.

"Why is someone sending you threats? You obviously took the intended and hoped-for action. You turned over the emails and got Denver in a heap of trouble. Why the harassment?"

"I—I do have an idea."

"I'm all ears." He curled his fingers around her hand in encouragement. Why would anyone threaten Martha Drake, a by-the-book CIA translator worker bee who'd reacted exactly as the sender thought she would?

"It might be because I copied all of the emails from my work computer to a flash drive, and now I have them at home."

Chapter Three

Cam Sutton's warm hand tightened around her fingers for a second. "Whoa. I bet the emailer wasn't expecting you to do that. Why *did* you do that?"

How could she explain it? She'd never done anything against the rules in her life. "I don't know exactly. There was something about those emails that didn't sit right with me."

"You said before that they might've been written by a foreigner." Cam tapped his temple. "You're a smart woman."

"I think it was the sentence structure and the word choice. Too formal or… I don't know what." She squared her shoulders and slipped her hand from Cam's. "When I first reported the emails, I tried to tell my supervisor about my suspicions, but he brushed me off."

"I take it nobody at the CIA knows what you did with those emails?"

"N-no." She pulled her bottom teeth between

her lips and traced the stem of her wineglass. Farah didn't count did she?

"You seem unsure. Did you tell anyone you forwarded the messages to yourself at home?"

"I didn't tell anyone anything."

"If someone's been following you and sending you poison-pen emails, somebody knows. Otherwise, they would've left you alone after verifying you'd turned over the messages."

"I don't see how someone could know I have the emails."

He hunched forward, and his energy came off him in waves and engulfed her, sweeping her up in his world. "You seemed hesitant before. Do you think your supervisor might suspect you?"

She snorted and took another swig of wine. "No way. If he did, he would've just reported me to security and gotten me fired…or worse. He wouldn't be hiring people to shove me onto the train tracks."

"You've got a point." He rubbed his hands together. "It has to be the party who sent the emails, the people who wanted to bring down Denver."

Her gaze dropped to his fingers drumming on the tabletop. "You're *glad* someone's after me."

"Wait. What?" He smacked his chest with

the palm of his hand. "That's dumb. I don't want to see anyone hurt over this."

"No, but you tracked me down because I'm the one who initiated the fall of Major Denver, and you probably expected some CIA drone that you could bully and instead you've discovered a chink in the story, a new twist you weren't expecting."

He cocked his head, and a lock of hair curled over his temple. He shoved it out of the way like a man accustomed to a military cut and whistled. "Are you sure you're just a translator and not an analyst?"

"*Just* a translator? I know four languages in addition to English." She ticked off her fingers. "Russian, German, French and Spanish."

"Okay, okay." He held up his hands. "You also have a big chip on your shoulder."

"I do not." She crossed her arms, covering her shoulders with her hands. "I'm just sick of being underestimated."

"Clearly." He leveled a finger at her. "And that's why you stole those emails."

"Are you sure you're *just* a Delta Force grunt and not military intelligence?" She held her breath.

He opened his mouth, snapped it shut and hit the table with his fist. Then he laughed, and what a laugh he had. A few heads turned at the loud guffaw.

"Shush." She kicked his foot under the table.

"Did those spies pick the wrong CIA drone to mess with or what?" He shook his head. "Why *do* you think they targeted you?"

"Honestly? I think they picked me because I have a reputation for following the rules. Everyone at work knows that."

"That's kinda scary."

"What? Following rules? You're in the military. You must do a lot of that."

"Not the rule-following, but the fact that the people who sent the emails knew that about you." He rubbed his knuckles across the sandy-blond stubble on his chin. "Inside job? Some kind of bug?"

"A few minutes ago you called them spies. Do you think this is some foreign entity or worse, a foreign country?"

"I don't know." He tapped her wineglass. "Are you done? I want to see those emails."

"You mean, at my place?" Her heart fluttered. It was one thing talking to this hunky military guy in public, but bring him back to her town house?

"You still don't trust me?" He slumped in his seat and finished off his beer. "What can I do to remedy that?"

"It's not that I don't trust you…exactly. I'm just not comfortable bringing strangers to my place."

He rattled off her address and winked. "I already know where you live, Martha."

"This is all really creepy. How long have you been following me around DC? Maybe my feeling of being tailed was coming from you."

"I swear, I just started following you from the Langley bus stop today."

"How do you even know about the Langley bus stop?"

"I have friends in high places."

She rolled her eyes. "Obviously not if you're dogging a lowly translator."

"I mean it." He grabbed her hands. "I want to see those emails. I know Denver. I'd be able to detect any falsehoods in those messages. I mean it's all false, but I might be able to see something in the emails, some clue."

An edge of desperation had entered his voice, and the easygoing frat boy had morphed into this earnest man with the serious blue eyes, desperate to clear his commanding officer's name.

Despite herself, she felt a twinge of pity and then steeled herself against the emotion. Her father had always employed the same tone when trying to wheedle compassion from her.

She blinked as Cam tugged on a lock of her hair. "C'mon, Martha. I saved you from an oncoming train. If you don't want me in your personal space, you can bring your computer out to someplace neutral, if you have a laptop."

She inhaled the fresh, outdoorsy scent coming off him and counted the freckles on his nose. Cam already *was* in her personal space, and she didn't mind one bit.

"All right. I'll take you back to my town house."

Cam waved at the waitress for the bill, and as soon as she plucked it from her apron, he snatched it from her fingers. "I'll get this."

Martha didn't even hesitate as she pulled a five and a ten from her wallet and flicked them onto the table. "That's too much like paying for information. I'll get my own wine."

Out of the corner of her eye, she could see Cam raising his eyebrows at her, but she ignored him and stashed her wallet back in her purse. "Is it all there?"

"Yes, ma'am." He tucked his bills and hers beneath the candle on the table, along with the check. "Walking distance?"

"You know my address." She folded her arms, regretting her decision already.

"I know your address, not the area, but I figured you were close if you got off at the

Metro stop." He pushed back from his chair and stepped to the side to let her go first.

As she shuffled past him, she noted his height again. At five foot ten, she hit eye level with most men, but her nose practically brushed the chin of this one.

When they reached the sidewalk, Cam hunched into his jacket and flipped up the collar against the wind. "It's not gonna snow, is it?"

"I hope not." She peered at the light gray sky and pulled on her gloves. "That would be pretty unusual for November."

They walked along the busy Georgetown sidewalk, occasionally bumping shoulders, which oddly reassured her, although she couldn't figure out why. Cam had the type of solid build that screamed strength and fitness. Physically, he could have his way with anyone, even a tall woman like her.

She hunched her shoulders and stuffed an errant strand of hair back under her hat. *Dream on, Martha.* Cam was the type of guy who'd wheedled homework assignments out of her. Just like in college, she had something he wanted—just not her body.

She stopped in front of the town house she owned but shared with a roommate, and grabbed the iron handrail. "I'm right here."

"Door right onto the street."

"Yeah? So what?" She fished her key from the side pocket of her purse, and for the first time in a while hoped her roommate, Casey, was on the other side of that door.

"Not that safe."

"If you haven't noticed, this is a nice area."

He looked up and down the street. "Lots of foot traffic though."

She looked up from turning the key in the lock. "I'm a very careful person."

"And yet, here I am."

She opened the door and blocked it with her body. "Are you telling me not to trust you? Because I can change my mind right here and now."

Casey yelled from the inside. "Close the door. You're letting in the cold air."

"My roommate. Protection." Martha jerked her thumb over her shoulder.

"Good thinking." He rubbed his gloved hands together. "Now can we go in? It *is* cold out here."

Martha pushed into the room, and Cam followed on her heels.

"I was just on my way…" Casey tripped to a stop in her high heels when she swung around and almost collided with Cam. "Well, hello there."

"Hey, what's up?"

"Casey, Cam. Cam, Casey, my roommate."

Casey stuck out her hand and wiggled her fingers, her long painted nails catching the light and glinting like she was casting a spell. "Nice to meet you. You're the first guy Martha's ever brought home."

The heat washed up Martha's face, and she ground her teeth together. "It's not like that. He's not a guy."

Casey fluttered her long—fake—eyelashes as she gave Cam the once-over. "You could've fooled me."

"I think what Martha means—" he hooked his arm around Martha's neck in a total buddy move and pulled her close "—is we're just friends."

"Of course you are." Casey turned toward the kitchen, giving Cam a view of her derriere in her tight dress. "Do you want a beer?"

"I thought you were going out?" Martha ducked out of Cam's hold and shed her coat.

"Just showing a little hospitality."

"Don't worry about it. He's *my* guest. I can get him a beer if he wants one."

"I'm good." Cam held out one hand as if refereeing an MMA fight. “We don’t want to hold you up, Casey. Nice meeting you.”

Her roommate’s pretty face fell, and Martha couldn’t help the little spark of satisfaction that flared in her belly. “Have fun, Casey.”

“Nice meeting you, Cam.” She swept up her coat from the back of a chair. “Hope to see you again sometime.”

The door slammed behind Casey in a gust of perfume and hairspray.

Cam cocked an eyebrow at her. “Not a good friend, I take it?”

“Not a friend at all, and she’s a horrible roommate—messy, noisy, brings guys back here all the time.”

“And you mean *guys*.”

“Yeah. She’s a real pain.”

“Move.”

“It’s my place.”

Cam’s gaze flicked around the town house, still sporting the expensive furnishings Mom had favored and she couldn’t afford to replace. “Government’s paying some solid wages.”

“Anyway, I can’t just move.” She had no intention of getting into her personal finances—or her notorious background—with Cam.

“Kick her out.”

“She signed a lease.”

“How long?”

"Four more months. I think she's gearing up to move out anyway."

"I'm sure you're counting the days." He clapped his hands once and she jumped. "The emails?"

"Do you want a beer? Or something else?"

"Just some water." He tipped his head at the door. "She doesn't know about the messages, does she?"

"Casey?" Martha snorted. "No. She wouldn't care, anyway. She's in DC to sleep around and maybe snag a book deal, and she has a good start on both."

"Who knew the capital was such a cesspool."

"I hope you're kidding." She strode into the kitchen and reached for a glass. As ice dispensed from the fridge, Cam joined her in the kitchen, making the space feel claustrophobic.

"I am kidding, and I'm convinced someone, somewhere in this cesspool has it out for Major Denver." He took the glass from her hand, his fingers brushing hers and giving her a jolt.

Leaning her hip against the kitchen counter, she tucked the hand behind her back. "Why would they have it out for him? Why frame him? By all accounts, he's a good soldier."

"The best and maybe that's why." He gulped down the water. "Maybe he stumbled onto something he shouldn't have."

"Again, that could point to a foreign entity."

"I agree, especially after what you told me about the emails, which are…"

"On my laptop." She brushed past him. "In my bedroom"

Leaving him in the kitchen, she jogged upstairs and pulled the door closed on Casey's messy room. She ducked into her own room, swept her laptop from the desk and tucked it under her arm. By the time she got downstairs, Cam had settled on the sofa in the living room, his long legs stretched out in front of him.

She sat next to him and opened her computer. "I put them in a folder on my hard drive."

"Where's the flash drive? You copied them to a flash drive when you stole them, right?"

She tapped the keyboard harder than she intended. "I didn't steal them. They were addressed to me."

"Addressed to your CIA address, but I'm not judging. Hey, I'm glad you did steal…take them, but where's the original flash drive?"

"It's in a safe in the office."

Raising his eyes to the ceiling, Cam asked, "This place has an office, too?"

"Yes." She zipped her lip and double-clicked on the folder holding the emails. "Is that secure enough for you?"

"I don't know if it's such a good idea to have

the messages in two places. You're doubling the opportunity for someone to take them."

"Why would anyone else want them? The CIA already has them." She pointed to her screen. "This is the first of the three emails I received."

Cam moved in closer and his warm breath bathed her cheek as he read the email aloud, slowly. "'Look at Major Rex Denver, Army Delta Force, and track his actions and communications. You will understand his behavior as treason. He has many contacts in region.'"

"Sounds stilted, doesn't it?"

"Wow." Cam slumped back and kicked one foot on top of her coffee table. "That's enough to raise suspicion and get you investigated? Good thing nobody ever sent the CIA information about my activities."

"There are two more emails with more details." Her hand hovered over the keyboard. "*Your* activities?"

"Not treasonous. I'm just saying stuff happens in the field, and it's better for everyone if it stays in the field." His hand dropped to her head, and he messed up her hair with his fingers. "Don't worry. I'm not doing anything to compromise national security—and neither was Major Denver."

She jerked away from him with a scowl,

smoothing her wavy hair back into place. "Do you mind?"

"Sorry. I have a younger sister, and I'm accustomed to teasing her." He tapped the keyboard. "Next email."

She huffed out a breath as she opened the second email. Great. The hottest guy she'd run into in months thought of her as a little sister. Typical.

Tipping the display toward him, she drew back and watched his profile as he digested the next message, his lips moving silently as he read it, his finger following the words. He must've read it a few times, as it took him a while to peel his eyes from the display. When he did, his jaw hardened and his eye twitched.

For all his carefree, easygoing ways, Cam really did care about Denver, and a strong desire to help him clear his commanding officer washed over her. She hated seeing anyone unfairly accused, and she'd had a feeling about these bogus emails ever since they landed in her inbox.

"Worse, huh?" She reached across him and opened the final email.

Cam took his time reading this one, as well, and when he finished, he punched the pillow next to him. "This is such garbage. All the CIA had to do was ask anyone who's ever served with the major. Even now nobody in the field believes Denver was conspiring with terrorists."

"Why'd he take off? Why didn't he just face the music and prove his innocence?"

"It's not supposed to work that way, is it? As a suspect, you don't have to prove anything. It's up to the prosecution to come up with the evidence to convict you. I'm guessing Denver recognized a setup when he saw one and figured the fix was in. There's no fighting against that when evidence is fabricated."

"He should've trusted the system." She jutted her chin.

"Really?" He bumped her knee with his own. "Like you did? C'mon, even someone like you knows there are times when the system breaks down and you have to take matters into your own hands."

"Even someone like me." She drummed her fingers on the edge of the laptop.

He cleared his throat. "You know, someone who likes to follow the rules…which is usually a good idea. I'm not knocking it."

"No offense taken. I have my reasons." She shoved the computer from her lap to the coffee table. "I'm just wondering how someone knew to target me."

"The CIA must've investigated the source of the emails. Let me guess. Fake IP address?"

"Yes, which they wrote off as coming from Dreadworm."

"So the sender got a bunch of CIA email addresses from Dreadworm, picked one at random and sent out these lies about Denver? I don't believe that for a minute, do you?"

"No, I think I was specifically targeted, but I don't know why I'm being harassed now. I did what the sender expected and wanted me to do." She shoved at her laptop with the toe of her boot.

"Because somehow they know you still have the emails, and they don't like that." He sat forward and dragged the computer to the edge of the coffee table. "You're not quite the good little soldier they anticipated."

"Serves them right." She grabbed Cam's water glass. "Do you want more water or something else?"

He held up one finger. "Does this LED light on your laptop monitor blink like this all the time?"

She squinted at the blue light at the tip of his finger. "I don't know. I guess so. Doesn't that just mean it's on?"

"Maybe, maybe not." He pulled the computer onto his legs and started clicking around.

"What are you doing?" She wrapped her hands around the glass. "Are you some kind of computer whiz, too?"

"No, but..." He dragged an icon from a system folder onto her desktop and turned toward her, his face tight. "This is a Trojan, and someone's watching you...us, right now through your computer's camera."

Chapter Four

Martha swallowed. Her gaze darted from Cam's blue eyes to the blue eye on her laptop. She snapped shut the computer. "How do you know that?"

"Shutting it solves the problem right this second, but that Trojan's gonna have to be removed from your computer as soon as possible. It's not just computer keystrokes and actions. The person on the other side can see you as long as your laptop is open and powered on."

"Oh my God." She covered her mouth. "I wonder how long this has been going on."

"A tech can probably tell you that by looking at the program. It'll have a date on it."

"But how did you know? How did you know where to look?" The veil of her preconceived notions about Cam Sutton lifted—and she liked what she saw even more. Brawn *and* brains.

"About a year ago, my sister was being

stalked." A muscle ticked in his jaw. "It became apparent that her stalker was watching her in her private moments. One of her friends, a real computer geek, came over to inspect her computer. First she watched for the blinking LED, and then she did a search for a common Trojan used to infect the computer and allowing an outside source to gain control of it. I looked for and found that same virus on your laptop."

Martha's mind raced and reeled over the times she'd had her laptop open in her bedroom, not bothering to shut it down. She hugged herself, digging her fingers into her upper arms. "Get it off. Can you get it off?"

"I can delete it. Hell, *you* can delete it, but I don't know if that removes it from everywhere. It's probably best if you take the laptop in or call someone to do it." Cam tapped his chin with his index finger. "I wonder if they could hear us, too."

"At least we were spared that. The microphone on my laptop doesn't work. No sound in. No sound out."

"That's an unexpected bonus." He hunched forward, digging his elbows into his knees. "Whoever was watching you saw me, but at least that person won't know who I am and how I'm connected to Denver."

She handed him the glass and pushed at his solid shoulder. “Put that in the sink or get yourself more. I’m going to open this up and delete that program. Then I’ll take my computer in and get the virus removed from everywhere else.”

Glass in hand, Cam pushed up from the sofa while Martha flipped open the laptop, keeping her thumb over the camera lens. She gasped and nearly drove her finger through her computer as a parade of skulls and crossbones marched across her display, the word *busted* floating between the grinning teeth.

Cam clinked the glass on the countertop. “What’s wrong?”

“Come and look at this. He knows I…you discovered the commandeered camera. He’s admitting he’s busted.”

“Son of a gun.” Cam hovered over her shoulder. “Cheeky bastard.”

“I wish I could just communicate with him and ask him what he wants. Oh.” Martha put her fingers to her lips as her email icon blinked, indicating a new message. “Maybe I can.”

“If you open that email, don’t click on any links. That’s how your computer gets infected. He might be trying to load something even more insidious on your laptop.”

"More insidious than a program to take over my camera to spy on me? That would be hard."

"Hold on." He backtracked to the kitchen. "Do you have any masking tape in here?"

"Post-its in the drawer to the right of the dishwasher."

He returned with two pink Post-it notes stuck to his fingertips. He slid a finger beneath the pad of her thumb, covering the eye of the camera with one Post-it and stuck the other on the edge of the first one to hold it in place.

"Go for it."

She opened the email and licked her dry lips.

"'Do you want to...play?'" Cam read the message out loud, which took off its sinister edge and made it sound almost sexy.

Of course, Cam could make anything sound, or look, sexy.

Dragging in a breath, she put her fingers on the keys.

"Wait." He cinched her wrist with his fingers. "What are you going to write back?"

"I'm going to write 'Hell, yes.' What do you think?"

"Shouldn't you ask him what he means? Ask him what he wants? That's what he'd expect out of you. If you agree too quickly, he's going to wonder if he picked the right person for the job."

His thumb pressed against her pulse. Could he feel it throbbing with excitement? She couldn't tell if the buzz claiming her body was coming from the email or Cam's warm touch. Did it matter? The two had mingled in her scattered brain.

Rotating her wrist out of his grasp, she said, "You're right. I'll take it slowly."

She voiced the words as she replied to the email. "'Play what? What do you want? Who are you?'"

She clicked Send and held her breath.

Her heart stuttered when the quick reply came through. She clicked on the email and read it aloud to Cam. "'I'm a patriot.'"

Cam snorted and she continued. "'I'm a patriot. That's all you need to know. You did the right thing. Leave it alone, or you might not like the game.'"

She whipped her head around to face Cam. "He's threatening me."

This time her hands trembled as she held them poised over the keyboard.

Lacing his fingers through hers, Cam pulled her hand away from the computer. "Ask this patriot why he's so nervous if the information he revealed in the emails about Major Denver is true."

"Shouldn't I ask him about his threats? If

he's the one who pushed me at the Metro?" She untwined her fingers from his.

"He's not going to give you a direct answer or admit that he tried to harm you, but I'm interested to see his lies about why he wants you to stop digging."

"I haven't even started digging." She puffed at a strand of hair that had floated across her face, and Cam caught it and tucked it behind her ear.

"He knows you saved the emails and shared them with me." He flicked his finger at the Post-its. "And he knows you're on to him."

"If you say so." As long as he kept finding excuses to touch her, she'd do just about anything he asked. She cleared her throat and her mind, and then typed in Cam's question.

They both jumped when a message showed up in her inbox, but it was an ad for ink cartridges.

"Come on, patriot." She flexed her fingers over the keys. "I think we scared him off."

"Or he's thinking up a good story." Cam stretched his arms over his head before standing up. "I'm going to get more water. Do you want something from the kitchen?"

"No, thanks." She wedged the toes of her boots against the coffee table. "We lost him."

"Do you think my question was too direct?"

He called back at her over the running water from the kitchen faucet. "We must've hit a nerve. He wants you to stop because he doesn't want the truth revealed—that the claims in those emails were all bogus."

Instead of an answer, grinning skulls danced across her screen, giving her the chills. "Ugh. He really is just playing games."

Cam returned to the living room and hung over the back of the sofa. "Idiot. I don't think he plans to tell you anything. He does want you to stop snooping though, and he's trying to scare you off."

"All the more reason to continue." She rolled her shoulders in an effort to release the tension bunching her muscles. "Maybe I should turn all this stuff over to the CIA."

"Martha, you committed a crime by making a copy of those emails. Even if you're not prosecuted, you'll lose your job." He reached past her and closed the lid of her laptop on the skulls. "It's not worth it. Do you want to wind up in federal prison?"

"No!" She dumped her computer from her lap to the sofa cushion. "You're right. I'm not telling the CIA a thing."

He drew back at the violence of her exclamation, but she didn't have to explain herself as the key turned in the door.

"Casey's home early." Her eyes wide, Martha watched the door handle turn and released a sigh when Casey crept into the room on tiptoes.

"Oh, you're still up…and *you're* still here."

The reason for Casey's dismay followed her into the room wearing an expensive suit and a sheepish grin. "Sorry to intrude."

"Join the party." Cam spread out his arms and then dropped them to his sides as his invitation was met with silence. "Just kidding. We were just wrapping up."

"Take your time." Casey circled one finger in the air. "Bob and I will be upstairs. Bob, this is my roommate Martha and her friend Cam."

They all managed awkward hellos and goodbyes as Casey led Bob up the stairs of the town house.

When she heard the door click above, Martha made a face. "She usually doesn't bring them home this early. I never have to meet them."

Cam whistled. "I can see why she doesn't."

"Why?"

Jerking his thumb at the ceiling, Cam whispered. "Old Bob up there is Congressman Robert Wentworth from some district down in Florida."

"What? Are you serious? How do you know that?"

"He's on the House Intelligence Committee—and he's married, as far as I remember."

"That makes it doubly worse that they're up there..." She waved a hand toward the staircase and heated up to the roots of her hair. "Why do women go for these married men?"

Martha flicked a glance at Cam's bare left ring finger and let out a little breath. Of course, lots of men didn't wear wedding rings.

"Imprudent of him at the very least." Cam leaned forward and lifted the laptop lid. "Still no communication from the patriot, so I'm going to head back to my hotel. Are you going to be okay?"

"I will be once I power down my computer and stick it in the office tonight."

"How many rooms does this place have?" He raised his eyes to the ceiling.

"Just three bedrooms. I could sublet the other room, but I'd probably go crazy with another roommate." She tucked the laptop under her arm. "Should I...should I call you tomorrow or something?"

"I'll go with you to cleanse your computer. Is that okay?"

More than okay. "Sure."

Cam strode to the kitchen and ripped a Post-it from the pad. He scribbled something on the pink square and then stuck it to the edge of the counter. "My number. Call me when you're ready to roll."

He grabbed his jacket from the back of the chair and hunched into it. "I'm sure I don't have to tell you to lock your door."

"Nope. I've got that one down. Besides, I have a US congressman upstairs for protection."

"All right, then." Cam stood in the entryway and thrust his hand forward for a shake. "Take care and thanks for trusting me."

She tucked her laptop against her side and took his hand in a firm grip—no nonsense. "Thanks for…rescuing me on the platform and discovering I'd been hacked."

They both released at the same time, and Cam saluted. "All right, then. See ya later."

Martha shut the door behind him and then rested her back against it, hugging her computer to her chest. Had Cam been nervous? Maybe he thought she'd expected a hug or a kiss or something. Did she appear that desperate?

She spun around and threw the locks into place and then launched herself up the stairs. Cam probably hadn't given her much thought at all.

Martha crept past Casey's bedroom door and the low voices murmuring within, and slipped into her own room. At least her master bedroom had a bathroom attached.

Tripping to a stop she glanced at the laptop in her hands. She didn't want to go into the hallway again, so she made an abrupt turn and stuffed the computer on the floor of her closet under some folded clothes.

She got ready for bed. Several minutes later as she slipped between the covers, her mind was still racing with the day's events.

Casey squealed from somewhere beyond the walls, and Martha burrowed beneath the covers. Her roommate and her lovers always made a lot of noise.

Martha reached into the top drawer of her nightstand for her earplugs and cupped them in her hand as the congressman let out a growl.

Shutting her eyes Martha closed her fingers around the earplugs. What would Cam sound like in the throes of passion?

Casey yelped, and Martha stuffed the earplugs into her ears as she buried her face in the pillow. One thing she *did* know is that she wouldn't be squeaking and squealing like Casey if she ever did get a chance with Cam.

And with that delicious thought making her shiver, Martha closed her eyes.

What seemed like moments later, Casey's

scream punctured Martha's dream state...and her earplugs. She groaned and rolled onto her side.

Didn't the woman have any shame—or self-control?

Casey screamed again, and Martha pulled the pillow over her head, gritting her teeth.

"Martha! Martha!"

The bedroom door burst open, and Martha sat up, the pillow falling from her face. She blinked her eyes at Casey standing in the doorway, a filmy nightgown clutched to her chest. Was she dreaming?

"Martha, wake up. We're in terrible trouble."

"What?" Martha flicked on the light above her bed, and Casey's face looked whiter than it had in the darkness. "What's wrong? What's going on?"

"Oh, Martha." Casey stumbled across the room and tottered before she dropped to the edge of Martha's bed. "Bob, Congressman Wentworth, is dead in my bed...in your town house."

Chapter Five

Cam glanced at his phone for about the hundredth time that morning. Maybe Martha had decided to get her computer wiped on her own. It's not like she needed him to do it. He didn't know that much about technical stuff, and she probably figured that out about him in a hot minute. She seemed like the self-sufficient type, anyway.

In fact, Martha Drake had a surprising rebellious streak. He never would've guessed she'd be the type to sneak out those emails. The woman had gone rogue—and he was glad she'd decided to do so.

And maybe she was going rogue again by handling the patriot herself. Cam wouldn't put it past her, but he didn't think it was a good idea. What if she'd fallen in front of that train last night? She needed a right-hand man, even if she didn't realize it yet.

He tossed his phone onto the cushion next

to him and snatched up the remote. Propping one bare foot on the table in front of him, he clicked over to one of the cable news shows.

He studied the reporters and news vans with a crease forming between his eyebrows. Someone had died, and the street where the buzzing media had gathered looked familiar with all those rows of town houses with shutters and arched windows.

When the words scrolled across the bottom of the screen, Cam choked and his foot slipped from the table. His thumb drilled into the remote to increase the sound.

The reporter breathlessly gushed into the mic. "All we know so far, Carrie, is that Congressman Robert Wentworth, from the Second Congressional District in Florida, died in this town house behind me sometime last night or this morning. There was a 911 call and the DC Metro Police responded. The body has not yet been removed."

Carrie put on a concerned face, but Cam could see the speculative light in her eyes. "Have the police said whether they're looking at foul play here, Stacie?"

"They haven't released any statement yet or talked to reporters."

Cam curled his fingers around the remote and hardly noticed the edges digging into his flesh. The reporter hadn't mentioned anything about anyone else being hurt…or arrested. What the hell had gone down in that town house after he'd left last night?

Cam muted the TV and reached for his phone. Damn that Casey for dragging Martha into her messy life. He stopped, his thumb hovering over the screen. Or was it the other way around?

Could this really be just a coincidence after what Martha had gone through yesterday? What possible connection could Wentworth have to Martha and the emails?

Cam dropped his phone when it hit him that he didn't even have Martha's number. He'd given her his number with the understanding that she'd call him to go with her to fix the laptop. Some understanding. Seemed like he didn't know Martha at all.

He paced the room, juggling his phone from hand to hand, occasionally turning up the TV for more news on the congressman's death. The stiff muscles across his shoulders began to unwind when he didn't see anything about any other injuries or anyone getting taken in for questioning, and then seized up again as Martha had been identified as the owner of the town house.

More than an agonizing hour later, Cam's phone buzzed with a DC number. "Hello?"

"Cam, it's Martha… Martha Drake."

"Yeah, I know. You're kind of famous right now, or at least your town house is. What the hell happened over there?"

"My name's out there, isn't it?"

"Are you worried about your job?"

"I'm worried about a lot of things right now." She sighed. "It looks like the congressman had a heart attack. Casey didn't even realize it until this morning. His body was slumped halfway out of the bed when she woke up."

"A heart attack? Of course, they're gonna do an autopsy before they rule on the cause of death." He wiped a hand across his mouth. "How are you holding up? How's Casey?"

"Casey is hysterical. I'm…nervous."

"Why, Martha?"

"Why do you think?"

"Are you linking this to the emails?"

"Aren't you?" Her voice rose, and for a second she sounded close to hysteria herself.

"Crossed my mind, but I can't see how this can be related to the emails or how it affects you." He wedged a shoulder against the window and watched one bare branch from a tree scrape against the edge of the balcony. "Heart attack, right?"

"Right." She cleared her throat. "We need to talk."

"And clean that computer."

"Don't come anywhere near here. It's a madhouse. I'll slip out the back and head over to your hotel. The police are still questioning Casey, poor girl."

He gave her the name of the hotel and the address before turning up the volume on the TV again. Several reporters were still camped out in front of Martha's town house, and the speculation had begun. Since Martha owned the town house, the reporters had her name on their lips.

It wouldn't be long before they dug up the fact that Martha worked for the CIA, and he hoped it wouldn't be long before they discovered she hadn't been the one who'd invited Congressman Wentworth to an after-hours meeting.

His blood percolated as he listened to the innuendo linking Martha to Wentworth, but he still couldn't figure out how this had anything to do with the threats from the patriot.

With the TV still droning in the background, Cam straightened his hotel room, stuffing clothes back into his suitcase and shoving toiletries into the plastic bag hanging from a hook on the bathroom door. He hadn't needed to see

Martha's place last night to figure she'd be a neat freak, and for some reason he wanted to assure her he wasn't a slob.

He went a few steps further and got a couple cans of soda from the vending machine down the hall and stuck them in the mini-fridge. The woman must've had a rough morning.

By the time Martha tapped on his door, Cam had rendered the room acceptable to the neatest of neat freaks.

He opened the door and she barreled past him without even a hello, striding to the sliding door to the balcony.

She turned to face him, twisting her fingers in front of her. "This is bad."

"Tell me what happened." He gestured toward the sofa facing the TV. "Not many details on the news, except that you own the town house where Wentworth croaked."

She perched on the edge of the sofa. "Casey's name will come out. The police are still talking to her."

"At least you won't be portrayed as the other woman for much longer." He yanked the chair back from the desk and straddled it, resting his arms across the back. "Give me all the details."

"After you left, I went to bed and I could hear those two…whooping it up." Two bright spots of red formed on her cheeks. "I have earplugs for just those occasions, and I was able to fall asleep."

"Damn, you need earplugs?" Noticing Martha's pursed lips, he wiped the grin off his face. "Go on. You fell asleep during noisy sex."

"I..." She ran her fingers through her messy hair, dragging it back from her face. "Yes, I fell asleep, and the next thing I knew Casey was in my room hysterical and crying, saying Bob had died sometime during the night."

"What time did she discover him?"

"About six. I ran into her room and felt his neck for a pulse. He seemed dead to me, but I have no experience in medicine. I called 911 right away."

"The news said possible heart attack, so I'm assuming no blood or visible injuries."

"No." Martha crossed her arms, cupping her elbows. "He was half out of the bed, as if he'd tried to get up but didn't make it."

"Did Casey have anything to say?"

"Not much to me, but the cops were grilling her. They'd met for a drink at a quiet place. Bob wasn't feeling great, and they decided to head back here."

"You'd never met him before? It didn't seem like you had last night."

"No. I'm not saying she's never brought him back to our place, but I usually make myself scarce when she brings guys home, so I'd never met him before."

Cam tugged on his earlobe. "I don't understand why you think some congressman's heart attack is related to you and the emails."

"Who says it's a heart attack?" She jumped up from the sofa and twitched back the drapes at the sliding door, peeked out the window and yanked the drapes back together.

"It could be something else. Poison. He didn't feel well. Or there are drugs out there that mimic heart attacks. Nobody would know the difference and *poof*—" she tried snapping her fingers, failed miserably and flicked them in the air instead "—you're gone."

Cam flattened the smile from his lips and drew his brows together to look concerned instead. He couldn't help it. Even when he listened to Martha talking about murder, he found her irresistibly cute.

"Wait, wait." He held up his hands. "How does that impact you, unless the patriot plans to frame you for Wentworth's so-called murder…and that's a long shot. How exactly does Casey's illicit affair with a politician affect you and your investigation of the emails?"

"It brings everything back up. It tarnishes me and anything I might have to say about these emails. It's a warning that he can get to me if he wants to." She pulled her bottom lip between her teeth.

"Yeah, okay. It shows he's powerful, although this is a risky way to do that. But—" he frowned for real this time "—what do you mean by bringing everything back up? Finding the emails?"

Her gaze darted to the TV, still humming in the background, and she took two steps toward the coffee table, picked up the remote and aimed it at the TV.

The reporter mentioned Martha's name, and Cam jerked his head toward the TV. A picture of a young Martha with thick glasses and braces stared back at him next to a picture of a gray-haired man who looked vaguely familiar. He tuned into the reporter's words.

"In a bizarre twist to this story, the owner of the town house is none other than the daughter of convicted stock trader Steven 'Skip' Brockridge, who's currently serving twenty-five years in federal prison for his role in a Ponzi scheme that bilked investors out of millions."

He twisted his head back toward Martha, her arms crossed and shoulders hunched. She raised one hand. "That's me, Martha Brockridge, daughter of a convicted felon."

Cam swallowed. "That's your father, not you. Obviously the CIA already knows about your background. A name change isn't going to throw off the Agency."

"I never tried to throw them off. I was up front about my father. They knew. I think they even believed that my father's criminal behavior had influenced me to follow the straight and narrow path, and they were right...until now."

Her voice broke at the end, and he jumped up from the chair and took her by the shoulders. He dug his fingers into her tight muscles. "This situation is completely different."

"Maybe, but do you think anyone's going to believe me about the emails now? A convicted felon's daughter?" She shook her head, and the ends of her hair tickled the backs of his hands.

"I doubt the patriot went through all this trouble to discredit or warn you, and the CIA already knows about your father. It didn't stop them from believing you the first time you turned over those emails."

"I don't know what to think. It's hard for me to believe there's no connection between my online conversation with the patriot and the death of Congressman Wentworth."

He blew out a breath. "I don't believe that, either. I don't believe in coincidences, but I can't wrap my mind around his motives."

"You think there might be another reason?"

He smoothed his hands down her arms and released her, stepping back. "How long has Casey been living with you?"

Martha blinked her long lashes. "About eight months."

"You received the emails four months ago, right?"

"You're not implying Casey is involved? That ditz?"

"It could've all been an act. The people who sent you the emails needed someone on the inside, and it would've been too hard to get one of your coworkers to cooperate. How'd that virus get on your laptop? I'm sure the CIA must drill computer security measures into your head and you didn't just click on some random link in an email. Who does that anymore?"

Martha chewed on the edge of her thumb. "I thought maybe he'd used Dreadworm again to get to me."

"How'd you meet Casey?"

"Through one of those roommate finders. She had the money up front—first, last and insisted on a larger security deposit than I'd asked for." She smacked her knee. "I should've trusted my instincts. I thought she was a little too eager."

"Something else about her choice in boyfriends." He straddled the desk chair again just to keep from touching Martha. It felt...manipulative to use her distress to get close to her. She didn't need any more distractions in her life right now, and neither did he.

"Congressman Wentworth?"

"Remember I told you last night I knew him from the House Intelligence Committee? He must have a lot of information on Denver."

She lowered herself to the bed as if in slow motion. "So, this is a twofer for Casey. She moves in to keep an eye on me, and she dates Wentworth to keep an eye on him and Major Denver."

"It makes sense that a lot of that stuff about Denver came from an inside source." Cam's anger at the injustice of Denver's situation burned in his gut. He crouched to grab the sodas from the fridge, cracked one open and took a long swig from the can. He held the other out to Martha, and she shook her head.

Tucking one leg beneath her on the bed, she said, "We're just guessing. How are we going to prove any of this?"

"Let's start with Casey. Where was she when you left?"

"She was still with the police."

"She'd admitted to the affair?"

"Of course. What other explanation could she give?"

"It's odd." Cam smoothed a hand across his freshly shaved jaw. "Why risk such public exposure? If Wentworth had served his purpose and they wanted to get rid of him, and maybe scare you in the process, why do it so publicly? They could've killed him without dragging Casey into the picture."

"You're asking me?" She jabbed a finger at her chest. "I still don't even know what the patriot wants of me, and I hate calling him that since he's clearly not one."

"I think he wants you to stop thinking about those emails for one thing and delete them. He wants you to drop your investigation."

"It's hardly an investigation, but I'm not dropping anything. People can't just get away with things." She pointed to her laptop case propped up against the wall by the door. "I called a computer repair place, and the guy told me to bring the laptop in today."

"You know this tech guy?" Cam stood up and stretched.

He didn't know how much longer he could be cooped up with Martha in this small room, anyway. He always had these instant attractions to women, and those never ended well, although Martha wasn't his usual type so maybe he'd learned a few lessons.

Her gaze flicked over his body as he reached for the ceiling, and then she took off her glasses and wiped the lenses with a corner of the bedspread. "He's worked on my computer before. He's good."

When she'd been checking him out, he'd had the crazy idea to flex and show off for her, but a woman like Martha would probably laugh at that. All the smart girls in school had him pegged as a meathead jock who couldn't even read. So he'd gravitated toward the pretty cheerleaders who only cared if he could read their flirtatious signals. He'd gotten good at that.

Coughing, he loped toward her laptop and hooked the case over his shoulder. "Have you checked your messages this morning for anything from the patriot?"

"It's one of the first things I did this morning after checking on Wentworth and calling 911—nothing."

He hunched the shoulder with the strap over it. "I'd find it hard to believe, but maybe this really is all a coincidence."

"You're right. Too hard to believe." She bounded off the bed. "My car's valet parked. We'll take that."

MARTHA DROVE HER hybrid like she did everything else—carefully and precisely. Cam felt like he'd wandered into the middle of a drivers' training video.

When she'd lined up the car perfectly between the white lines of a parking space in a mini-mall, she cut the engine and glanced at his profile. "What?"

"What, what?"

"Why are you grinning like that?"

"Nice parking job."

She huffed through her nose and swung open her car door.

The computer tech in the store didn't blink an eye when Martha walked up to the counter. He either hadn't seen the news yet about Congressman Wentworth croaking in Martha's town house, or he was trying to be polite.

Martha plunked her laptop on the counter and spun it around to face the techie. "Hi, Marcel. I've been hacked, invaded, compromised, whatever you want to call it."

"Ooh, a Trojan?" Marcel flipped up the lid and widened his eyes when he saw the Post-its blocking the camera. "Dude got to your camera?"

"Yes, he's been watching me." Martha wrinkled her nose. "So creepy."

"And pretty sophisticated." Marcel stuck

some tape over the camera lens and plucked off the Post-its. "Any idea who your stalker is?"

"No. Just get rid of it." Martha gripped the edge of the counter. "You can, can't you?"

"Oh, yeah." He nodded toward a computer in the corner humming through some diagnostics. "I'm working on that one, but I can get yours started. You can wait. There's a pretty good Thai place two doors down."

"That sounds good. I'm starving." Martha's gaze darted to Cam's face. "I mean, if you want to get something to eat while we wait."

"Absolutely." Cam peeked out the window through the blinds. "It's already getting dark. I had breakfast at the hotel but completely skipped lunch."

"I guess that's settled." She turned to Marcel, waving a slip of paper. "Do you need my password?"

"Honestly, I can get past it, but I'll do it on the up-and-up." He took the paper from her between his two fingers and lifted the laptop from the counter to take it to a station in the back of the shop.

Cam beat Martha to the door and opened it for her. "The restaurant is to the right. I noticed it when we drove into the parking lot. I already knew I was hungry."

She stuffed her hands into her pockets as

she headed into the blustery wind, listing to the side.

"Are you going to get swept off your feet?" Cam placed a hand on her arm.

"No." She dropped her eyes to his hand, and he released her.

"For a minute there I thought you were going to take off with the wind." He felt like he needed some kind of excuse for touching her again.

When they entered the empty restaurant, the waitress on the phone behind the counter waved them into one of a dozen tables scattered around the room.

"I guess we're too late for lunch and too early for dinner." Martha shed her coat and folded it onto a chair at a table by the window.

Ten minutes later, they waited for their food while Martha blew on her hot tea and Cam tipped his beer into a glass. "That must've been rough on you when your father was arrested. You were a teenager?"

"Yes. It couldn't have happened at a worse time."

"Yeah, those awkward teen years, and then you have to deal with notoriety on top of it all."

Her eyes met his briefly and then seemed to search his face before moving in a slow inventory down his neck, chest, across his shoulders and down his arms.

Her study of him felt like a caress, exploratory and featherlight.

Then her brows snapped over her nose. "*You* had awkward teen years? Not likely."

He smiled and his jaw ached with the effort. "We all have our issues. What was your father's crime? Securities fraud?"

"Something like that." She waved her hand. "It's confusing, but it boiled down to cheating and scamming. He was always good at that."

"How long is he in for?"

"He's been in for ten, and he's eligible for parole in about five more."

"Do you see him?"

"Occasionally."

"He must've made good money—legitimately—at one time."

"He did quite well for a number of years. I did the whole private school thing, and when I started showing an aptitude for languages, he arranged for language schools and tutoring."

"He must've been proud of you."

"The feeling was not mutual." She rubbed the back of her hand across her nose. "What about you? Where are you from? How long have you been in the military?"

"I enlisted when I was nineteen, after one

year in college playing football." He tapped his glass and watched the bubbles rise and try to break through the thick head of foam blocking their escape.

One disastrous year when he couldn't keep up academically, no matter how many tutors the coaches sent his way, and flunked out, losing his football scholarship. "Yeah, the military was a good fit, and it didn't take long before Delta Force started looking my way."

"You must be something special. That's an elite unit."

"It suits me."

The waitress interrupted them with several plates of steaming food, and as Martha removed her glasses, Cam raised his eyebrows.

"The food is fogging up my lenses."

Martha looked cute in glasses, but without them her eyes mesmerized him as they seemed to shift in color and glow like a cat's in the low light.

The soft pink that crept into her cheeks gave him a jolt. He was staring at her like an idiot. She probably dated educated guys with multiple degrees and witty conversation.

"Do you want some rice?" He held up the round container of sticky white rice. *Real witty, Cam.*

For the rest of the meal, they danced around

each other, sharing little bits of information about themselves. Cam took his cues from Martha, skimming across the surface of his life and allowing her to fill in the blanks.

He tried to fill in her blanks, too, but she'd perfected the art of the dodge. Maybe she'd learned that from her old man, even though she seemed to reject everything he stood for.

Her cell phone buzzed on the table beside her plate, and she flicked a grain of rice from its display before she tapped it. Her lips pursed as she read the text. "You're not going to believe this."

Cam's pulse jumped. "What? It's not the patriot, is it?"

"No, it's Casey. She wants to meet me—away from the town house. She has a lot of nerve."

"You're not meeting her alone." Cam pushed his empty plate to the middle of the table. "She might be involved in Wentworth's death up to her eyeballs."

"She says she wants to apologize and discuss moving out. She doesn't want to go back to the town house now that she's been outed as Wentworth's mistress."

"Where is she?"

"At a hotel not far from yours." Martha tapped her phone to reply to Casey's text.

"She wants to see you now?"

"As soon as I can get over there."

Cam checked the time on his own phone. "Let's pick up your computer before the shop closes, and then we'll head over there—together."

"I told her to give me an hour." She grabbed her glasses and put them on, peering at him through the lenses. "You're serious? You're coming with me?"

"Like I said—" he reached for his wallet "—I don't trust that woman. And don't tell her I'm coming along. We'll surprise her."

"I didn't mention you, but I still think you're wrong. Casey is too flakey to be some international spy." She plunged her hand into her purse and withdrew her wallet.

Cam's gaze dipped to Martha's hand, pulling out some cash, and he swallowed. No woman he ever dated expected to pay, not that he'd allow it, but this really wasn't a date, and a woman like Martha might be offended if he insisted on paying.

He waved the check. "Uh, fifteen bucks each, but I'll throw in twenty since I had the beer and you had tea."

"Whatever." She tossed a ten and a five onto the table. "I'll pitch in for your beer in exchange for your protection…from Casey. She might poke me with her stiletto or shoot me in the face with hairspray."

"Go ahead and scoff. Congressman Wentworth trusted her and look where that got *him*."

They walked back to the computer store and picked up Martha's newly cleansed laptop. She did a quick check of her emails before putting it away.

As Cam stashed the computer case in the trunk of her car, Martha said, "Now if the patriot wants to contact me about Wentworth's death, he'll have to find another method."

"If he really wants to contact you again, he will. He already has your email address. He doesn't need to watch you."

Martha drove back into DC toward a hotel a few blocks away from his own. She paid for guest parking in the structure beneath the hotel, and they rode up in the elevator to the fifth floor.

As the doors opened and they stepped onto the thick carpet, Martha whispered, "Maybe she wants to tell me what really happened to Wentworth."

"If she didn't tell you in the time you two were waiting for the ambulance, why would she be coming clean now?"

She shrugged, and they turned the corner in the direction of Casey's room. Cam trailed behind Martha just in case his appearance in the peephole scared off the woman.

But he didn't have to worry about a peephole. Casey had propped open the hotel door with the latch, wedging it between the door and the jamb.

Martha raised her brows at him as she knocked on the door and called out. "Casey?"

No response.

"Maybe she stepped out and wanted to leave the door open for me." Martha placed her hand flat against the door. "Casey? It's Martha."

A tingle raced across the back of Cam's neck, and he pulled his gun from his pocket.

Martha jerked back when she saw it. "What are you doing? Where'd that come from?"

"My pocket." He put a finger to his lips. "Shh."

As Martha pushed open the hotel door, Cam followed closely on her heels. Nothing about this felt right. He flicked the lever back and pulled the door closed.

A lamp in the corner illuminated the empty space, a suitcase open on the bed, a curtain billowing into the room from the open door to the balcony.

"Casey?" Martha crept to the closed bathroom door and pushed down on the handle, swinging it open.

Cam hovered behind her.

Martha gasped and choked. She stumbled against him.

He caught her around the waist and peered over her shoulder.

His gut churned as he took in the sight of Casey in a tub of red-tinted water, one hand hanging over the side, pointing at the pool of blood on the tile floor.

Chapter Six

All at once, the smell flooded Martha's nostrils, the metallic taste filling her mouth. She gagged.

Cam dragged her backward out of the bathroom and propped her against the wall while he dashed toward the sliding glass door, his weapon raised.

She blinked and slid down the wall, her legs crumpling beneath her. Where was he going? Was he cold? She was cold. A ferocious shiver had gripped her body, making her teeth chatter and her hands shake.

The cold had crept into her limbs and she couldn't move them, couldn't get up. Cam had left her, had disappeared out the sliding glass door, had left her alone with… Casey.

Oh, God. Maybe Casey wasn't dead.

It took all Martha's concentration to hunch forward onto her hands and knees and turn toward the open bathroom door, but she remained rooted to the carpet, rocking back and forth like a baby learning to crawl.

"Martha!" Cam scooped her up as easily as if she were a baby and wrapped his arms around her, holding her back against his front. "You don't need to go back in there. Casey's dead."

"H-how can you know?"

"The blood, the..." He walked backward, towing her along with him, and settled her on the edge of the bed. "Stay here. I'll check."

As Cam left her again, her knees began bouncing up and down. She clasped her hands over them and pressed down, digging her heels into the carpet.

Cam returned and crouched in front of her, taking her stiff hands in his. "She's gone."

"Did she drown? I don't understand. Did she slip and fall? Where did all that blood come from?" Her voice began to rise, and she clamped a hand over her mouth to stop the panic burgeoning in her chest.

Cam brought her hands to his lips and kissed her knuckles. "She slit her wrists, Martha."

"No. Oh, no." She shook her head back and forth so hard, her glasses slipped down her nose.

"We have to call 911 and the hotel." Cam

pocketed his gun, pulled his sleeve over his hand and picked up the room's telephone.

He murmured into the receiver, hung up and placed another call. Then he walked to the door of the room and wedged it open the same way Casey had left it for her.

Martha watched all his actions, the fog starting to lift from her brain. Casey was dead in the bathtub—a suicide.

Minutes later, a hotel security guard and a hotel manager burst through the door.

Cam pointed to the bathroom. "She's in there. I already called 911."

The two hotel employees crowded at the bathroom door, and the manager screamed, "Oh my God!"

Cam pulled Martha up from the bed and wrapped her in a hug. He whispered in her ear, "Are you okay? Still in shock?"

Her lips moved against the rough material of his shirt, but she didn't make a sound. She cleared her throat and tried again. "Why would she do that?"

He squeezed her tighter and she closed her eyes, breathing in the scent of him. She never wanted to leave this safe place.

All too soon, the police and EMTs surged into the room and the questions started.

Of course the police had heard of Casey Jessup, the DC intern who'd been too hot for the congressman to handle.

They questioned Martha about her presence here at the hotel, Casey's demeanor, her motives. They hauled some booze and pills out of the bathroom, items Martha hadn't even noticed.

Cam handled everything calmly and confidently, subtly protecting her by moving closer whenever the cop's questioning veered toward the intrusive.

After what seemed like hours, the nightmare finally wound down. Casey's body was still in the bathroom, but the police were letting them leave. The officer had her number and would call if they had any more questions or needed to visit the town house and search Casey's things.

She and Cam said nothing as they walked out of the room, but he entwined his fingers with hers on the way to the elevator. When the doors of the car closed behind them, he let out a long breath.

"I'm sorry you had to go through all that, sorry you had to stay in that room. I would've hustled you out of there and made an anonymous 911 call, but I'm sure the hotel has cameras that would've caught our arrival and departure, and the cops may even be checking

Casey's cell and would've identified that text going to your phone number."

He'd released her hand, and she threw it out now to brace against the mirrored back of the elevator car. "We couldn't have left. We found her. Th-that's like leaving the scene of a crime."

"A crime?" He stabbed at the elevator button again.

"Technically, suicide is a crime, isn't it?" She sagged against the elevator wall and twitched when it landed in the parking garage.

As they exited onto their level, Cam held out his hand, palm up. "I'll drive. You're still shaken up."

Biting her bottom lip, Martha rummaged through her purse and pulled out her key chain. She dropped the keys into his hand, and he opened the passenger door for her.

She plopped onto the seat and snapped her seat belt, keeping a tight hold on the shoulder strap. When Cam slid behind the wheel and started the engine, she turned to him. "Why did you go outside to the balcony? What were you doing out there?"

"Why'd she leave that door open?"

"Maybe she was enjoying a last breath of fresh air."

"The police think she may have taken an

overdose of pills with some alcohol for good measure. Did she think slicing her wrists in the bathtub wasn't going to do the trick?"

"What did you see on the balcony?" Martha trapped her hands between her knees and trapped the air in her lungs as she held her breath.

"A way out."

"Do you think someone else was in that room?"

"Why did Casey text you? We were there an hour later. You're telling me she drank that vodka, took those pills, climbed into the bath and slit her wrists all before we got there?"

Martha spoke up over the roar building in her head. "She drank the booze and popped the pills before she contacted me. She thought maybe I'd get here before she was dead, so she decided to speed up the process."

"Why would she do that, notify you, I mean? The two of you weren't even close." He hunched over the steering wheel, crossing his arms on top of it. "I could see that original text. She didn't want to go back to the town house and wanted to give you some kind of notice that she was moving out. Maybe she even wanted you to help her out by packing up her stuff and shipping it to her. But why would she want you here at her death?"

Martha lifted her shoulders to her ears and held them there. "She didn't want a loved one or a close friend to find her, but she wanted *someone* to find her."

"Do you really believe Casey was so distraught over Wentworth's death that she offed herself in commiseration? If anything, a girl like that would've relished the attention, gotten a book deal, landed on reality TV. You told me that's what she was all about."

Martha rested her head against the cool glass of the window. "You think she had help. You think she was murdered."

"C'mon, Martha. Use that logical mind of yours—emails, threats, a dead congressman in your place and now Casey's so-called suicide. All coincidence?"

"It all seems so random."

"It does, but I guarantee you, it's not. This is all connected somehow."

"Do you think the police will figure it out? What about those hotel cameras? If they would've caught us, they would've caught Casey's…killer."

"Unless he snuck over that balcony or disabled the cameras."

"I'm scared, Cam."

He reached over and squeezed her knee. "Get rid of those emails. Forget this whole thing."

"What about Major Denver?"

"We'll figure out a way to help him. Hell, he's probably helping himself."

"Oh, no." Martha pressed her nose to the window and took in the reporters still hovering on the sidewalk outside her place. Her breath fogged the glass. "I can't go through that. Wait until they find out this latest news."

Cam ducked his head and swore. "Vultures. Don't they have more important stories to report on? Is there a back way into your place?"

"They discovered it already." She tucked her hands beneath her thighs. She didn't want to be alone in that town house. Didn't want to leave Cam.

"You should stay in a hotel tonight." Cam flexed his fingers on the steering wheel. "If you want, you can stay in my room."

"That would be great…if you really don't mind." Had she just guilted him into that invitation? Did he see her as the poor, little friendless nerd? "I mean, I can call a friend if it's too much trouble."

The car lurched forward, and he squealed away from the curb. "I think it's better if you stay with someone who knows what's going on right now—someone with a gun."

She twisted her head to the side. "You really think I'm in danger."

"Martha, I don't want to freak you out right now, but I have my doubts that Casey killed herself. I have my doubts she even texted you."

"That balcony. You think someone was waiting for me out there?"

"I think he heard us talking at the door. He wasn't expecting you to have company, so he took off." Cam flicked on the wipers and rubbed the inside of the windshield with his fist.

"He could've shot me…us as soon as we walked into the room." She watched a drip of water on the outside of the window join up with another one and then another to form a little stream.

"Who said he had a gun? Who said he wanted to kill you? We don't know what the patriot wants."

"According to you, he killed Casey. Why would he do that?"

"She knew too much."

"I know more than she does."

"She knew the right things." He swung into the driveway in front of his hotel and left the keys with the valet.

As they entered the lobby, Cam pointed to the gift shop next to the elevators. "Do you want to pick up a toothbrush and whatever else you might need?"

After her shopping spree, Martha dangled the plastic bag from her fingers as she and Cam made their way to his room. She'd rushed here this afternoon convinced Wentworth's death had something to do with the emails about Denver. Now another death had been added to the mix, and she wasn't sure about anything anymore—except Cam.

He had her back—whether from pity or his strong desire to use those emails to clear Major Denver, she didn't know and she didn't care. She'd bask in the safety of the protective aura that wafted around him.

He opened the hotel door for her and gestured her through. "Sorry it's not a suite, just the one room. You can take the bed and I'll camp out on the sofa."

Her gaze swept the length of the truncated sofa—almost a love seat—and then scanned Cam head to toe. "You're not going to fit on that thing. I'll sleep there."

"I've slept on worse than that." He held up one finger. "Don't argue with me."

She raised her eyebrows. "I hadn't planned on it. I'll take the bed, and you don't have to twist my arm. And I'll even lay claim to the bathroom first."

"Be my guest." He dragged a pillow from the bed. "I will take one of these."

"Be *my* guest." She twirled the plastic bag of toiletries around her finger and tripped to a stop at the bathroom door. "Do you have a T-shirt or something I can wear to bed?"

"The ones in the closet are all clean. Help yourself."

Martha reached into the closet and yanked a gray T-shirt from a hanger. She made for the bathroom and closed and locked the door behind her—not that she expected Cam to make a raid on the bathroom while she was in here undressing.

Bracing her hands on the vanity, she hunched toward the mirror. Her flushed cheeks and bright eyes were signals of the adrenaline that had been pumping through her system nonstop all day as she bounced from one crazy event to the next.

At the end of it all she'd wound up in the hotel room of this hot Delta Force D-Boy, who had zero expectations of her. And why would he? She'd helped guys like this with their homework and papers many times in college, and they'd never demanded anything from her except the guarantee that she'd help them again.

She let out a long breath and brushed her teeth. She took off all her clothes except for her bra and underwear, and pulled the T-shirt over her head.

Cam's extra-large T-shirt billowed around her tall, thin frame, hitting her midthigh. It would sweep a tinier woman's knees, but she'd never been a tiny person. Tall, gawky and awkward had marked her teen years.

She folded her clothes into a neat pile. Clutching the bundle to her chest, she crept back into the room.

Cam jerked his head up and jabbed at the TV remote, but not before she heard Congressman Wentworth's and Casey's names.

She placed her clothes on a vacant chair. "They're on that like a pack of dogs on a rabbit's scent."

"Until the next scandal breaks." He tossed the remote onto the bed. "Did you have everything you needed in there?"

"I did. Your turn."

As Cam disappeared into the bathroom, Martha turned on the TV but skipped all the news channels. She *was* the news for the second time in her life. She didn't have to watch it. Settling on a nature show, she bunched the pillows behind her and settled back.

Ten minutes into the program, Cam eased open the bathroom door and poked his head around the corner. "Are you still awake?"

"After the day I just had, I'm wired. I'm going to need a few more hours of watching plants grow in fast-motion before I can even think about sleeping."

He stopped in front of the TV and shook his head. "That would put anyone to sleep."

He turned off the lone light in the room, the tall lamp next to the sofa, and grabbed the hem of the white T-shirt he'd been wearing beneath his denim shirt, pulling it up.

Martha got a quick glimpse of his six-pack, illuminated by the blue light from the flickering images on TV, before he pulled the T-shirt over his head and she averted her eyes.

As he unbuckled his belt, she shoved her glasses up the bridge of her nose and studied the insects hatching on the screen. And she hated insects.

Yanking down his jeans, Cam turned his back to her and she turned her gaze onto him. His pants dropped down his powerful thighs, and Martha swallowed at the sight of his muscled buttocks in the black briefs.

He kicked his jeans into a corner and then shot her a look over his shoulder.

She cleared her throat and pulled a pillow into her lap. Had he caught her watching him undress?

"Guess I should try to keep the room neater with two people in here."

She waved her hand. "Do whatever you'd normally do."

He walked to the discarded jeans and picked them up. As he draped them over the back of a chair, he said, "I don't think you mean that."

"Sure I do. I don't want to upset your routine."

He cocked his head. "Really? 'Cause I usually bunk in the buff."

A flood of warmth washed into her cheeks. "I—I mean, if that's what you..."

He held up his hands and flashed that boyish grin that pretty much did her in. "Don't worry. I'm not a perv."

What if she admitted she wouldn't mind one bit if he stripped down completely?

"And I'm not a complete prude, you know."

"Prude? I never thought you were." He crawled into the bed he'd made from the sofa, propping his head on the arm of it. "What did I miss?

"We don't have to watch this if you don't want." She held out the remote into the space between bed and sofa. "Just no news."

"As long as we're both awake, how about you mute this fascinating look at mating insects and we talk instead?"

She squinted at the image on the TV. "Is that what they're doing? I think they're just eating."

"Whatever. Can we talk about what happened today? I know you think Casey was too stupid to be involved, but I think you're wrong."

"Stupid? I didn't mean to imply that Casey was stupid. She's flakey. *Was* flakey." Martha pulled her knees to her chest with one arm.

"Maybe flakey Casey was putting on an act, or maybe they used her, used her flakiness."

"You mean perhaps she was a legit roommate and they got to her *because* she was my roommate, instead setting her up to be my roommate?" Martha rolled her head to the side to face Cam, resting her cheek on her knee.

"That's exactly what I mean." He curled one arm behind his head, bunching up his biceps. "She moved in with you, and they approached her with an offer."

"And Congressman Wentworth? How does he fit into the picture?"

"Maybe once they had her hooked, they told her to target him. She was a beautiful woman. Wentworth already had a rep for inappropriate sexting. It wouldn't have taken much for a girl like Casey to get her claws into him."

Of course, he'd noticed Casey's attractiveness. Had he compared her to her sexy roommate and found her wanting? Her sexy, *dead* roommate.

Martha drew her bottom lip between her

teeth. "Do you think they killed her to tie up loose ends? To keep her from talking?"

"Those would be a couple of reasons."

"Why would they, or *he* if we're just talking about the patriot, want to lure me to Casey's hotel room to discover her body?" Martha stretched out her legs, pulling the pillow up to her chin. "Another warning? They got what they wanted from me originally. I turned over those emails to the proper authorities. Now they want me to leave well enough alone. That's the only motive I can figure out."

"It's a strong motive." Cam yawned and slid farther beneath his blanket. "So, why don't you?"

"Leave it alone?" She clicked off the TV and rolled to her side. "Maybe I will."

Of course, if she deleted the emails and let the patriot know what she'd done and put all her efforts back into her job at the Agency, she'd never see Cam Sutton again.

And she didn't know if she could give him up just yet, danger or not.

THE FOLLOWING MORNING, Martha sat up and squinted against the weak wintry light slipping through the drapes.

Cam yanked them closed. "Sorry."

"That's okay. What time is it?"

"Almost seven. You can go back to sleep if you want. You had a long day yesterday that turned into a longer night."

"I'm awake." She eyed his fully dressed form by the window and rubbed her eyes. And her dream had ended. "It might actually be a good time to drop by my town house and collect a few things. The press might still be sleeping, or maybe some celebrity couple got a divorce overnight and Wentworth and Casey are no longer the hot news."

"Collect your things?"

Cam's gaze darted wildly around the room as if assessing how all her stuff was going to fit in here.

"Don't worry." She whipped back the bedcovers and swung her legs over the side of the bed, tugging on the T-shirt with one hand. "I'm not moving in here. I can relocate to my mom's place."

"Where's that?"

"Maryland."

"She lives here, and you haven't called her yet with all this going on?"

"Her house is here. She's in Florida with her new husband."

"Has she called you? She must've heard about Wentworth dying in your town house—even in Florida."

"She texted me, asked if I was okay and went on with her life."

"She's all right with you relocating to her house?"

"She suggested it." Martha jerked her thumb over her shoulder. "I'm going to shower here."

"Do you want breakfast before we leave?"

"No." Her head jerked up. "We?"

"I'm not letting you back into that lion's den by yourself. You can collect your stuff, drop me off here and hole up in your mother's house." He whipped open the drapes. "And think about letting this go."

She nodded before ensconcing herself in the bathroom. She showered and dressed in record time. The sooner she got away from Cam, the easier it would be to forget about him whether she wanted to or not. And she didn't want to.

She snorted softly as she turned her back to the warm spray from the showerhead. There was going to be nothing easy about getting Cam out of her mind.

An hour later, she drove up to her place, Cam in the passenger seat beside her. One news truck had taken up residence across the street, but the hordes of reporters and cameras had taken a break.

"We're in luck." She parallel parked half a

block down from her place. She kept her head down as Cam took her hand and pulled her along quickly to her front door.

As she used her key to open the door, she sucked in a breath. "I need to get Casey's extra key from its hiding place before I leave."

Cam followed her closely into the town house. "That's risky, keeping a key like that. I hope it's not under the welcome mat."

"No. It's a good hiding place." She dropped her key chain into her purse and hung it on a peg by the front door. "Casey was always forgetting her keys or losing them, so I stashed an extra for her just in case."

Cam surveyed the room. "At least the police didn't designate this as a crime scene."

"They did search Casey's bedroom and bathroom, but there were no injuries on Wentworth's body, no evidence of foul play. Looked like a heart attack, but we both know there are ways to mimic that with a drug."

"We'll let the police figure that out. Pack up and let's get out of here before the hyenas gather."

"I thought they were vultures..." She put her foot on the bottom step of the staircase and turned. "You can help yourself to whatever if you're hungry."

"I plan to buy you breakfast." He nodded toward the TV. "I am going to take a look at the news though."

"Knock yourself out. I won't be long."

Once in her room, Martha rolled a suitcase from the closet and started packing for her workweek. What would Gage have to say to her about this weekend?

She hadn't done anything to jeopardize her security clearance—at least nothing Gage knew about.

She finished up with her toiletries from the bathroom and even threw in a couple pairs of disposable contacts. She wore them occasionally, even though they dried out her eyes by the end of the day. Wanting to wear contacts had nothing to do with Cam.

She'd dragged her suitcase into the hall and rolled it to the top of the staircase when Cam came bounding up the stairs.

"I'll help you with that." He picked it up by the handle and carried it down as if it were empty. "Is that everything?"

"What I don't have, I can come back for or buy. Mom has more than enough at her place."

She plucked her purse from the peg and balanced it on top of her suitcase. "I'm just going to get that key, and I'll be ready. Have the vultures started circling yet?"

Standing to the side of the bay window in the front, Cam peeked through a gap in the drapes. "Nope. I'll come with you to get the key."

"It's out back in the garden." She crossed through the kitchen and turned the dead bolt on the back door.

She stepped onto the pavers, kept dry from the recent rains by an awning over the patio. Then she crouched next to a patio chair with a plastic cover and pulled back the zipper on the cover about an inch. She shoved two fingers inside, probing.

When she found the key, it had some paper wrapped around it. "This is weird. Maybe it's the tag from the chair cover."

Cam kneeled beside her. "Did you find the key?"

"I did, but there's some paper wrapped around it." She pinched the key and the paper between two fingers and pulled it out.

She tipped the key into her palm and unwrapped the scrap of paper. Her heart flipped in her chest and she gasped. "She knew. She left me a note. Casey left me a note."

"What does it say?"

Martha read the words from the slip of paper that shook in her hand. "'If anything happens to me, talk to Tony.'"

Chapter Seven

Cam caught Martha's shoulder as she started to tip over. She'd almost been clear of this mess.

"Who the hell is Tony?"

Martha pressed her fingertips to her temples. "I'm not sure. There have so many men since Casey moved in. Tony. Tony."

The rain started up again, pinging the fiberglass awning above them. He took Martha's arm. "Put that away and let's get out of here."

Martha shoved the note and key in her pocket and turned toward the town house.

While she locked up, Cam flicked the edge of the drapes aside and peered out. "They're back. Get ready to do the duck and dodge."

She grabbed her purse from the top of her suitcase and slung it over her shoulder. "Maybe I can use my suitcase as a battering ram through the crowd."

"Don't worry about your bag. I'll handle

that. Just put your head down and make a beeline to the car."

They faced the front door, and as he grabbed the handle Martha put a hand on his wrist. "Thanks for helping me out, Cam."

"Since I kinda got you into this mess, it's the least I can do."

"Even if you hadn't shown up when you did, this patriot person would've still taken these actions. Maybe I would've been dead beneath the wheels of that oncoming train two nights ago."

"I'm glad you're not." He pressed a kiss on her forehead and opened the front door.

The media sensed movement, smelled blood and swarmed around the front porch. They shouted Martha's name, Casey's name, Wentworth's name. Cam couldn't make out any of the questions—not that Martha would be answering them anyway.

He put his arm around her shoulders and charged down the sidewalk to her car, dragging the suitcase behind him. He breathed into her ear, "Get in the driver's seat and start the engine. As soon as I get in the car, take off."

Martha hurried to the car, ten feet away, and unlocked the doors. She scurried around to the driver's side, and Cam lifted the lid of the trunk and swung the suitcase inside. As he slammed it shut, she started the car.

He strode to the front passenger door, and someone touched his back. "Who are you? Martha's boyfriend?"

Cam growled, "I wish," and slammed the door in the reporter's face.

"Hit it."

She peeled away from the curb, her eyes on the rearview mirror. "Don't they ever get tired? What do they hope to gain from sitting in front of a building?"

"They just got it—a shot of you hauling your suitcase out of there." He clicked his seat belt in place. "What about Casey's family. Do you know if they've been notified?"

"The police contacted her mother and sister last night. I've never met them. Casey never talked about her family, but I told the police to give them my contact information when they get to town and I'll let them into the house." She hunched her shoulders. "What awful news."

"And now we know it's murder."

"We should tell the police, give them the note."

"Do you think Tony's going to be willing to talk to the police? Do you think he wants to expose Casey if she'd been doing something illegal?" He rubbed his eyes. "That's if we can even figure out who he is."

"I know who Tony is."

"You do?"

"I remembered when we were running down the sidewalk. He's a bartender. Through all the guys, he's pretty much been a constant fixture."

"Last name?"

"I don't know, but he works at a bar in Georgetown. I'd just need to call to see if he's working tonight."

Her phone buzzed in the cupholder where she'd stashed it, and Cam glanced at the display. "It's the DC Metro Police. Do you want to answer it?"

"Yeah. Speaker."

He tapped the phone for her and put it on Speaker.

"Hello?"

"Ms. Drake, this is Detective Merchant with DC Metro. I have a couple of questions for you about Ms. Jessup."

"Go ahead. I'll try to help." She raised her brows at Cam.

"Have you been back to the town house you shared with Ms. Jessup?"

"I have."

"Did she leave a suicide note there or any

indication what she was planning? We didn't find any notes at the hotel."

"No notes."

Her jaw tightened, and Cam knew what it cost her to lie to the police.

"Also, do you know what keys she had on her key chain?"

"No. Why do you ask?"

"We didn't find a key chain or any keys at all in her personal belongings or in her purse—just her wallet, some makeup, her cell phone. Did she have a car?"

"No car, but that seems weird she didn't have her house key, at least." Martha turned her head to meet Cam's gaze.

The officer cleared his throat. "Not so strange if she wasn't planning to return to the town house."

"Y-you're right. Do you know if her family is coming to DC to collect her personal items?"

"They'll be in touch and so will we. That's all for now, Ms. Drake."

"Okay, thanks."

Cam ended the call for her. "That's not good, Martha."

"The keys?"

"Exactly. Who has them? Maybe those attack reporters staking out your place saved you from an unwanted visitor last night. If the person who killed Casey took her key, he now has easy access to your place…and you."

"I'll get the locks changed."

"Good idea." He patted his growling stomach. "How about that breakfast I promised you?"

"I don't feel like going out. We can eat at my mom's place if we stop for some groceries on the way. Is that okay with you?"

He tipped his head. "Are you worried about being followed by the patriot, or you're afraid people will recognize you from TV?"

"Do you think he's following me?" She grabbed the rearview mirror and adjusted it.

"I've been watching." He rapped his knuckle on the window toward his own mirror. "Nobody has been following us, not even the press."

Slumping back in her seat, she said, "I just don't want people staring at me. I had enough of that when my dad was arrested."

"I'm more than happy to eat a home-cooked breakfast at your mom's, but I don't think you have to worry about people recognizing you. That picture the reporters keep flashing of you on TV must've been from a while ago." His gaze lingered on her face and hair. "You look different."

"That picture was from my late teenage years, years I just wanted to disappear."

"I can see that from the picture. You wore bigger glasses, baggy clothes and your hair practically covered your face." He reached out and tucked a loose strand of hair behind her ear, his fingers hovering at her earlobe. "I like it this way better—where I can see your face… your eyes."

She coughed and pinned her shoulders against the seat. "Maybe my appearance won't inspire a paparazzi frenzy, but I'd still rather eat in."

"You got it." He dropped his hand. "I'll even cook, if you like something simple like bacon and eggs."

"Simple? Bagels and toast are about the most complex I get in the morning. You know how to cook?"

"I know the basics."

"I'm impressed."

Cam lifted his chin and smiled. He couldn't help it if Martha's praise stoked his ego. Somehow meeting this woman's approval had become a priority for him.

After a stop at a grocery store, Martha headed east until she hit the coast and then turned north, where Cam caught glimpses of the bay between big houses and rolling lawns. Guess the government hadn't forced Skip Brockridge to give back all the money he swindled.

Martha wheeled her car into the circular driveway and pulled up in front of the double doors.

Cam whistled. "Nice digs. Does she have a bay in her backyard?"

"A bay and a boat dock." She threw the gear into Park. "But no boat."

"Cutting costs?"

"The boats were always my dad's thing—his and mine." She rubbed the end of her nose and exited the car.

He followed her to the trunk and hoisted her suitcase out. He balanced one of the grocery bags on top while Martha snagged the other two. "Did you grow up in this house?"

"This dump?" She swept her arm across the expansive, light blue clapboard front with the wraparound porch. "Mom did have to readjust when Dad was sent to prison, downsize. I don't even know why she bought on the bay. It was never her thing."

"Is there someone here? It doesn't look abandoned."

Martha plucked a key from her key chain and swung it back and forth. "Not right now, but Mom's housekeeper comes in once a week to dust mostly, and the gardeners keep up their weekly schedule."

"You said your mother was in Florida?"

"For the winter—like a bird." She unlocked the dead bolt and shoved the key into the handle to finish the job.

Cam followed her inside, dragging her suitcase behind him, his head swiveling from side to side. "Do you share a decorator with your mother? Looks similar to your place."

"The town house was my mother's, from my grandmother. I can afford to live there—with a roommate—but I can't afford to redecorate."

"Do you want this upstairs?" Cam rolled the suitcase to the foot of a curved staircase.

"You can leave it for now." She held out the two grocery bags. "Let's put you to work in the kitchen."

Cam widened his eyes as he stepped into the kitchen, the copper pots hanging above a center island catching the light and reflecting off the shiny granite counters, lined with enough appliances and gadgets to stock a cooking show. "This is way beyond my capabilities."

"If it's beyond yours, you can imagine how I feel walking in here and pouring my cereal in a bowl." She placed the groceries on the island and then rolled up the sleeves of her sweater. "Tell me what to do."

He held up a finger. "You always wash your hands first. That's what my mama taught me."

"Did your mother teach you how to cook, or did she and your sister baby you and you had to learn on your own later?"

"My mom baby me?" He snorted. "She was a single parent, worked nights a lot so I had to fend for myself."

"Oh." She paused, hugging the carton of eggs to her chest. "What happened to your father?"

He bumped her hip so he could wash his hands at the sink. "My dad took off when my sister Lexie was a baby and I wasn't much older. We never saw him again."

"I'm sorry."

"I'm not. From all accounts he was a bastard, and we were better off without him."

"Funny, I thought..." She shook her head. "Bowls are in that cupboard. I'll leave the egg mixing to you, and I'll start cutting some veggies and grating the cheese."

He lodged his tongue in the corner of his mouth as he cracked several eggs into a bowl. What had she thought about him? At least she'd given him some thought.

"Milk?"

She opened the fridge and pulled out the carton she'd just put away. Looking over his shoulder, she asked. "Do you want me to pour it in? Just tell me when to stop."

He continued whisking. "Okay, pour, little more, little more. Stop."

She put away the milk and tipped her head back to survey the pots swinging above them. "I don't even know which one would work for an omelet."

He reached over her head to grab a pan. "This one will do."

"Is this enough for the filling?" She held up the cutting board for his inspection.

"I've never heard omelet ingredients called filling before, but that'll work."

"I told you I didn't know my way around a kitchen."

"Let me guess. You had a cook."

"We did." Her mouth tightened. "All bought and paid for with ill-gotten gains, but my mother liked to cook. She must've been thrilled when she had a daughter because Mom enjoyed all those typically feminine pursuits, but I was interested in…other things."

"Boating?" The butter sizzled in the pan as Cam swirled it around and up the sides. "I figured you must've spent most of your time holed up with books and studying."

"Oh, the boating." She shrugged. "I did that because *he* liked it."

"Your father."

"Uh-huh." She sniffled. "Too much onion, I think."

"It's fine." Her sniffling had nothing to do with onions. She'd acted like she hated her father before, but that couldn't be further from the truth.

He finished off the first omelet and tipped it onto a plate. Then he constructed the second, messing up the corner when he flipped up the one side.

"I'll take the defective one."

She twisted off the cap of the orange juice bottle and poured two glasses. "They both look perfect to me."

"We didn't get coffee." He slid the damaged omelet onto the second plate with a flourish.

"I'm okay without it."

She carried the glasses to the center island and placed them at the corner of the place mats. He followed her with the plates and centered them on the mats, trying to match her perfection.

"I don't need coffee. I think I'm too wired as it is." She pointed to her laptop case on the coffee table. "I haven't even checked my messages today. What if my friend has some news for me?"

"Unless he can tell you he's going to leave

you alone or tell you what he wants from you, his news is worthless." He shook out the cloth napkin next to his plate and draped it over one knee. Martha had brought them back to reality, so he might as well jump in with both feet. "Are you going to call Tony's workplace later to see if he's on tonight?"

"Yes, but I wonder what he knows. Why wouldn't he tell the police or why wouldn't Casey have warned *him* to call the cops if anything happened to her?"

"Maybe she didn't want to involve him." He cut off a corner of his omelet and waved it at Martha. "She warned you instead because you're already involved."

"Great." She poked at her eggs. "This looks really good. I'm sorry I brought up the other stuff. I don't want to ruin your appetite."

"Mine?" He stabbed a mushroom. "Not possible."

They continued chatting, avoiding the issues front and center, and Martha told him about growing up in the Chesapeake Bay area. Her upbringing couldn't have been more different from his on the hardscrabble streets of Atlanta, but the most glaring difference involved father issues. He had no desire to even find out where his was, and Martha had clearly idolized hers—until he'd disappointed her.

No wonder she didn't have a boyfriend on the scene. She must've set her standards high after the fiasco with her father.

They finished breakfast, and Martha insisted on cleaning up since he'd done the cooking.

"You can do the dishes, but I have to help. My mom ingrained that into me, and she'd smack me upside the head if she found out I let someone else do all the cleaning."

"Your mother still lives in Georgia?"

"Yeah, and I can't get her to leave the old neighborhood." He shook his head. "I keep trying to get her to find another job and move, but she claims she doesn't do the physical work like she used to."

"What does she do?"

"For years she worked as a maid at a hotel. She's still at the same damned place, but now she's the housekeeping supervisor." He shrugged. "She won't give up that job."

Martha dried the plate in her hands and then folded her arms around it, clutching it to her chest. "She worked hard to support you and your sister."

"That she did."

"She must be proud of you now."

"She says she is."

As she stacked the plate in the cupboard,

Martha twisted around to stare at him. "She *says* she is. You don't believe her?"

A knot twisted in Cam's gut. "She didn't go to college, so she really wanted me to go. I had a football scholarship to pay for it and everything, but I just couldn't hack it. Couldn't get through those classes."

She turned away from the cupboard and leaned her back against the counter. "Ah, the good-looking jock couldn't find someone to do his homework for him?"

His gaze darted to her face and she flinched, blinking her eyes behind her glasses. Was that what she thought of him? Easy for her to make judgments with all this privilege and the brains to go with it.

"I wouldn't know." He slammed the dishwasher door. "I never tried to get someone to do my work for me. Just tried to do it myself—and failed miserably."

Curling her fingers around the edge of the counter behind her, she said, "I-I'm sorry. I didn't mean…"

"Sure you did." He ground out a laugh. "Girls like you, so superior."

She shoved off the counter and grabbed his hand with both of hers. "It's not even about you, Cam. It's all about me and my shortcomings."

"*Your* shortcomings." He rolled his eyes, but

her hands, warm and soft from washing the dishes, squeezed his, and his tight jaw started to relax.

"It's just that you reminded me of all the hot guys in high school and college who used me to do their homework and write their papers, and then completely ignored me in every social setting. Guys I'd studied with all semester would look right through me at the next frat party, and I kept telling myself I wouldn't help them anymore, but I always did. It was one small way to fit in, and I desperately wanted to fit in."

He licked his lips and searched her face for any sign of deception. Her incredible eyes shimmered with tears, and he saw a woman who trusted him enough to be honest and open.

"Those guys were idiots, but even if I'd had a girl like you helping me every night, I still would've flunked out of school."

"I don't know about that. I was a pretty mean tutor back in the day."

"I'm sure you were, but I wouldn't have been able to concentrate with you sitting across from me."

Her eyebrows shot up, and now it seemed to be her turn to study his face. "You're serious."

"Damn straight."

Red flags flew in her cheeks, and she wrinkled her nose. “I’m still sure I could’ve gotten you through.”

“Naw, and it’s no reflection on your talents.” He twisted his hands out of her grasp and placed them on her shoulders. “I couldn’t handle school because I’m dyslexic. I thought you’d noticed before. I can barely read.”

Chapter Eight

Martha put a hand to her heart, which Cam's words had just pierced. "I'm the idiot."

He rubbed his thumbs against her collarbone. "You didn't know."

"Yes, but the assumptions I made about you." Her hand crept to her throat. "I feel like such a fool, and I'm so sorry for stereotyping you as the dumb jock. Like I said, I'd been humiliated by plenty of them. And honestly? It probably wasn't even their fault. They didn't twist my arm to help them. I gladly did it to bask in their...hotness."

Cam tipped back his head and laughed at the ceiling, breaking the tension between them although she wasn't sure she wanted it broken. That tension had been building for a while, and she'd assumed it was all one-sided...hers, but he'd called her a distraction. She'd never been someone's distraction before.

"Take it from the dumb jock. You intimidated those dudes. They're used to admiration not admonitions."

"When you say things like that, you don't sound dumb at all. You need to stop calling yourself that." She pressed both hands against his chest. "You have to know that you wouldn't be a member of one of the most elite special ops teams in the military if you were all brawn and no brain."

"I'll make you a deal."

Her fingers curled against his shirt. If she could keep standing this close to him forever, she'd be willing to make a deal with the devil himself. "What kind of deal?"

"I'll stop referring to myself as a dumb jock if you stop referring to yourself as a geek, especially with that tone of voice you use when you do it."

"Do I?" She dropped her eyelashes. "Have a tone of voice when I call myself a geek?"

"You do." He brushed his knuckles across her cheek. "And I don't like it."

"Should we shake on it?" She made no move to remove her hands from his chest, and he hadn't released her shoulder yet.

His gaze dropped to her mouth, and a pulse throbbed in her lower lip. So much better to seal it with a kiss.

Her phone went off, and she almost sobbed

with frustration when Cam jerked his head to the side.

"You'd better see who that is. Whoever used Casey's phone to text you yesterday now has your number, and I'm sure he's going to take advantage of that."

She broke away from the already broken spell and lunged for her phone, ready to scream at the person on the other end. She drew her brows over her nose when she recognized Gage's number from the office. "My boss is calling me on a Sunday?"

"Do you mind if I listen in? It might have something to do with the emails."

She tapped the phone to engage the speaker. "Hello? Gage?"

"Martha, I'm here with the section chief, Rand Proffit."

She swallowed the lump in her throat. "Hello, Mr. Proffit."

"How are you, Martha? Pretty rough weekend."

"Yes, it's been crazy. I had no idea my roommate was…dating Congressman Wentworth. If I had, I would've reported it."

She drove a fist into her belly. Would she have reported it? Was that any of the Agency's business? Did she owe them anything?

Proffit's voice reassured her over the phone,

like some creepy, condescending uncle. "I'm sure you would have, Martha. I know we can count on you to always do the right thing, but this whole situation has put us in an interesting and unfortunate position. One of our employees, someone with a questionable past of her own caught up in a sex scandal involving a ranking member of the House Intelligence Committee. Doesn't look good."

"Sex scandal?" She ground her back teeth. "I'm not involved in any sex scandal."

Cam had been moving closer to her and now he hunched over the counter, a scowl marring his handsome features.

"Of course you're not, but all that was taking place in your town house…under your nose."

"Hardly under my nose. They were in another room with the door closed." Heat flared in her cheeks as she recalled eavesdropping on the sounds of their lovemaking through the walls and across the hall.

Proffit clicked his tongue, or was that her moronic boss?

"We're not blaming you in any way, Martha, nor are we holding you accountable." He cleared his throat and she held her breath. "However, we're putting you on a leave of absence for the time being—just until the whole situation dies down—and it will be paid leave. So, think of it as a vacation."

"I have work to do."

"Farah can take over." Gage couldn't hide the glee in his voice.

"Farah doesn't speak Russian."

Gage had a ready answer. "We'll get someone in the department to handle your work, Martha. Don't worry about that."

She gripped the phone so hard she thought the screen would crack. "When this…situation dies down, my job had better be waiting for me when I come back, or you'll answer to my attorney."

"Are you going to use your father's attorney?" Gage snorted.

"Damn straight." She ended the call and tossed the phone across the counter.

Cam whistled. "That's the way to handle 'em. They're so sure of you, aren't they? I'd like to see the looks on their faces if they ever discovered you took charge of those emails."

Her anger backtracked to fear, prompting her to worry her bottom lip with her teeth. "They can't ever find out. I'd lose my job and probably wind up in a cell next to my father's."

"They're not gonna find out from me." Cam walked around to her side of the counter and patted the stool between them. “Sit down. You look ready to collapse.”

She perched on the stool and folded her hands in front of her. “Gage would like nothing better than to get rid of me.”

“I noticed. What’s that guy’s problem?”

“He’s afraid I’m going to take the job he wants.” She twisted her fingers. “He probably doesn’t have to worry about that anymore.”

“If we can get enough proof that those emails were lies, you’ll be right in line for that promotion.” He patted her back and then strode toward her laptop abandoned on the coffee table. “Are you ready to take a look at your cleaned-up computer?”

“At least my cleaned-up computer won’t be looking at me anymore, although now that the patriot and I are like this—” she crossed her fingers “—he’ll probably feel free to email me. I’m sure he got my home email address, thanks to Casey the unlikely spy.”

“Maybe he’ll be kind enough to tell you what the hell he wants.” Cam slipped her laptop out of its case, brushed a few crumbs from the place mat and set it down in front of her.

She wiggled her fingers before powering up the computer and entering her password. “If he admits to killing Casey or Wentworth, I’m turning him in. I don't care what the ramifications are for me."

"Even if he admits it, we don't know who he is. Is he one person? A group? Is he the same person who pushed you at the Metro station?"

Her shoulders stiff, she launched her email and watched the messages populate on the screen. She eked out a breath with each email she scanned and discarded. "Nothing from him."

"Maybe he's done with you. Showed you the reach of his power, got rid of a few loose ends and figures you've been adequately warned to let the emails implicating Major Denver drop."

She shoved the laptop away from her. "We're still going to see Tony tonight if he's working, aren't we?"

"Of course."

"Then he figured wrong."

AS LUCK WOULD have it, Tony Battaglia still worked at the Insider in Georgetown, and he had a shift that night.

Cam insisted on babysitting her at her mom's house the rest of the day, and she didn't put up much of a fight. She made sandwiches for lunch, her one culinary accomplishment, and they both worked on their laptops until she took him out back for a walk along the shore of the bay.

She'd had an online conversational Russian class that afternoon, but she couldn't tell what Cam's work involved, and she didn't want to ask. He'd requested a quiet place to listen on some headphones and speak into a mic, so she invited him into her mother's library, which was really her father's library since all the books had belonged to him.

She'd shown Cam where to plug in and then had gotten out of there as fast as she could. The sight and the musty smell of her dad's books served as a reminder of all she'd lost when he decided to play fast and loose with the rules.

Like she was doing now.

When they'd come in from their walk, the cold had reddened Cam's cheeks and the breeze had ruffled his light brown hair, giving him the appearance of a model for a men's magazine on the great outdoors. She had a hard time reconciling his Adonis good looks with the insecurities he'd shared about his dyslexia.

Her heart ached for that part of him, while her body ached for the other part. She couldn't have ordered a more perfect hero than if he'd come special delivery from central casting.

As he removed his coat, he said, "No more of this eating in. We'll go to out to dinner on our way to the Insider—and I'm paying. You've had to put up with me hanging around all day."

The only negative to having him hang around all day was that he was in a different room from her.

She shrugged out of her coat and dropped it on the sofa. "That works for me. I'm going to shower and change. Do we need to stop by your hotel on the way so that you can do the same?"

He brushed his hands over his faded jeans and stomped his work-style boots. "Yeah, I definitely need to clean up."

"Help yourself to anything in the kitchen." She waved her hand in the general direction. "And you can carry on with…whatever you were working on before."

"Reading."

"What?"

"I was working with a reading program. I try to keep at it whenever I'm on leave. If I'd had this program when I was younger, it would've helped a lot."

"That's admirable."

He ducked his head and his cheeks got redder. "I wasn't fishing for praise."

"I know that." She spun around not wanting

to embarrass him anymore. "Well, get to work then, and I'll get ready for dinner."

Several minutes later as Martha stepped into the shower, a smile played about her lips. She hadn't felt this connected to a man ever.

She stepped beneath the warm spray and by the time she emerged, she'd lost the smile. What she and Cam had didn't come close to real life. She felt close to him because he'd become her protector, her lifeline in a crazy sequence of events that had just spun out of control. He felt close to her because he liked playing the protector.

If he hadn't come on the scene and all this stuff had gone down, she'd probably be sitting in a police station right now confessing everything. He'd naturally assumed she wouldn't go to the police, and she'd gone along with him on this roller-coaster ride—just like she'd gone along with her father even though she'd discovered his crimes long before the FBI had come knocking on their door.

She ended her shower far from the dreamy state she'd been in at the time she cranked on the water. She yanked her towel from the rack and gave her skin a harsh rubbing. She'd fallen into her old patterns. Some hot guy with a boyish grin crooked his finger at her, and she'd been ready to do his bidding.

But it wasn't exactly his bidding. Cam had saved her, had been there for her, protected her. That all made this a different experience completely.

Buoyed by her renewed justification of events, Martha leaned close to the mirror and popped in her contact lenses, blinking rapidly after she inserted each lens. Nothing out of the ordinary about wearing contacts. She usually chucked the glasses when she went on dates.

She finished getting ready, and then slipped out of the bathroom into the connecting bedroom. She'd already laid out a pair of black skinny jeans and some tall black boots. Pulling a teal sweater over her head, she tugged it into place and resisted the urge to pull at the shoulders to bring up the V-neck. She patted the neckline, which was a long way from plunging.

She put on the finishing touches with a blow-out of her hair and a heavier than usual application of makeup. She wanted to present a different appearance from the one plastered all over the news—at least that was her story and she was sticking to it.

She rested her hand on the bannister as she took one step at a time in her high-heeled boots. By the time she reached the bottom,

Cam was there to meet her, his eyes as wide as his grin.

"You look...great." He held out his hand to help her off the last step.

"Thanks." She fluffed the ends of her wavy hair. "I figured I should disguise myself a little just to keep a low profile."

"Uh-huh." He lifted one eyebrow. "Good idea, but I'd hardly call that look low profile. You're gonna have all eyes on you in that getup."

"Too much?" She placed a hand flat against her tummy.

"For a night out in Georgetown? Nope. For me? Not at all."

She moistened her lip-sticked mouth. She hadn't fooled Cam at all with this supposed disguise. She'd dressed for him and had gotten exactly the reaction she'd craved—and she didn't feel silly or nervous or uncertain at all. She felt beautiful because he made her feel that way.

"Are you ready?" She held up a small black bag. "I'm just going to switch purses."

"I'm ready. My laptop is all packed up." He pointed to the front door. "I took the liberty of making sure everything was locked up down here. How come that security system wasn't engaged when we got here?"

"Mom's housekeeper leaves it off because she keeps forgetting the code."

"Do you know it?"

"Yes."

"Engage it tonight and leave it activated for as long as you're staying here. You can always call the housekeeper and give her the code."

She looked up from shuffling things from one purse to another. "Is that why you stayed all day? You're afraid I'm vulnerable here?"

"The guy, or guys, killed a congressman and his mistress. I'm not taking that lightly even though we still don't know what he wants from you."

"I agree. Give me two minutes."

While Cam waited by the door, Martha set the alarm system for the house. When she joined him, she said, "All done."

"Better safe than, well…you know."

When they got to his hotel, she insisted on waiting at the bar while he went up and changed to spare them both the awkwardness of having her watch over him while he showered and changed.

"I need a glass of wine anyway."

"Okay, I won't be long." He wagged a finger at her. "Don't talk to strangers."

His warning gave her a little chill, but she

laughed it off. "I'll be here when you come back down."

She slid onto a stool at the bar and barely glanced at the scattered couples at the tables. She ordered a glass of red wine from the bartender and took a deep sip, closing her eyes as the warmth spread to her muscles.

"Long day?"

Her eyelids flew open, and she turned her head in the direction of the male voice beside her. "You could say that."

"Same for me." He raised his glass of whiskey. "Travel day. Those are the worst."

"Let's see." She held up her hand and ticked off her fingers. "Lobbyist, congressman back from a home district visit, attorney. Shall I keep guessing?"

"You do know this town." He swirled the amber liquid in his glass. "Lobbyist."

She laughed and fluttered her eyelashes, which seemed to act as some kind of invitation to the stranger. They spent the next half hour exchanging witty repartee. She didn't even know where half the stuff out of her mouth was coming from.

"You know, Martha, you've already made my travel day one hundred percent better. Can I buy you dinner?"

"Oh, I'm sorry." And just like that she'd led

someone on even though she hadn't meant to. "I'm meeting a…friend for dinner. In fact, here he is. Nice talking to you, Alan. Have a good week."

Alan cranked his head over his shoulder in time to see Cam making his way through the bar and muttered, "Lucky bastard. Have a nice dinner, Martha."

She met Cam halfway through the bar and nodded. "You clean up nicely."

Cam jutted his chin and glared over her head. "Was that guy trying to pick you up?"

"Just passing time." She took his hand. "Until the main event."

"I don't blame him." Cam interlaced his fingers with hers and did a U-turn to exit the bar. "I figured you wouldn't be flying under the radar looking like a million bucks."

Martha lengthened her stride to keep up with him, noticing a few other admiring glances thrown her way. She flipped back her hair and straightened her spine. Cam could go on about her looks all night, but she understood the difference.

Cam's attentions had given her confidence, and even the plainest girl in the room could command the spotlight exuding confidence.

Even with her newfound assurance, Martha rejected a trendy Georgetown restaurant for a quieter place serving Italian food in a homey atmosphere.

Once they each had a glass of red wine and a basket of bread between them, Cam hunched forward, crossing his arms on the table. "What's our strategy with Tony? Have you ever met him?"

"He's probably the one guy Casey *didn't* bring home, not that I saw much of the others. I swear, running into Congressman Wentworth that night was a rare occurrence." She tapped a fingernail against her glass. "But if Tony's some kind of confidante of Casey's, I'm sure he knows about me or at least knows my name. Why would she blab secrets to a bartender?"

"Are you kidding? Most bartenders probably hear more of people's problems than therapists do." He tore off a piece of garlic bread and pointed it at her. "You're just going to march in and introduce yourself?"

"I'll start slowly and then hit him with the note I found. Who knows? Maybe he's expecting it because Casey told him she'd be calling him out as some kind of witness if anything happened to her."

"I hope he doesn't plead the Fifth. If it's not crowded in the bar, maybe we'll have a chance to talk to him while he's on the job, or at least make arrangements to talk to him later."

When the waitress arrived with their food, Cam pointed to Martha's glass. "Do you want another?"

"No. I want to have my wits about me tonight, and I already had half a glass at the hotel. That first night after the incident on the Metro platform? Those two glasses of wine were my limit. You wouldn't want to see me after a third."

"Wanna bet? Don't get me wrong. I admire your…restraint, but I can't help wondering what an out-of-control Martha would look like."

"I don't—" she cut off a corner of her spinach lasagna "—let myself go."

"You should try it sometime. It's good for the soul." He broke off another piece of garlic bread. "You should also try some of this bread before I eat it all."

She watched his fingers as he brushed them together, dislodging crumbs into the napkin on his lap and wondered what it would be like to let go with Cam. She was no virgin, but all of her sexual encounters had been very measured and controlled. Probably her fault.

For the rest of the meal they didn't talk any more about losing control or Tony or Casey or the congressman. It was as if this dinner represented a deep breath, a chance to step away from the crazy before plunging back into it headfirst.

They finished their food and, true to his word, Cam picked up the check. As he placed some bills on the tray, he said, "Are you okay to drive?"

"I think so, although I usually don't drive at all after I've imbibed."

"When it comes to drinking and driving, you can never be too careful." He held out his hand. "I'll take the wheel."

"You've had a glass of wine, too."

"I'm twice your size and drank half as much."

"You have a point." She fished her keys from her purse and dropped them into his cupped palm. "You know where you're going?"

"It's not far from here, right? You can be my navigator."

When they reached the bar, Cam pulled up to the valet parking attendant and left him the keys. As they walked in, Cam ducked to whisper in her ear, "Do you have any idea what Tony looks like?"

She nodded to the bar where a man and a woman were mixing and pouring drinks. "Easy. He's the man."

"At least it's not crowded." He tipped his head toward one of the TVs over the bar displaying photos of Wentworth and Casey. "I wonder how Tony feels about that playing 24-7 in here."

"I guess we're going to find out soon enough."

They claimed two empty seats at the bar, the nearest customer three stools down.

The female bartender got to them first. "What would you like?"

"I'll have one of these." Cam held up a cardboard coaster printed with the name of a bottled beer.

"Club soda with lime for me, please."

Martha tilted her head back and followed the muted images parading across the TV screen. Even without the sound she could piece together the story—or maybe that was just because it was *her* story.

When the bartender set their drinks in front of them, Cam handed her a folded ten and asked, "Is that Tony Battaglia?"

The bartender's gaze flicked from Cam to Martha, two small lines forming between her eyebrows. "Yes. Do you have business with him?"

"Business?" Cam's hand jerked and a dab of foam leaped over the edge of his mug and rolled down the side. "We have mutual friends."

The woman's scowl deepened.

Martha added, "Just when he has a minute."

"I'll let him know." She snatched up Cam's bill and spun away.

Cam lifted one shoulder. "Weird."

"Okay, so that wasn't just me?"

"Definitely an odd reaction. Maybe the media made the connection between Casey and Tony and have already swooped in for a comment or reaction."

"That's probably it." Martha swirled the straw in her glass, clinking the ice against the sides.

From the corner of her eye, she saw the bartender say something to Tony. He glanced their way, but his face didn't change expression. They waited another ten minutes and three customers before Tony meandered over to them.

He whipped a towel from his waistband and wiped the clean counter next to them. "We have a mutual friend?"

"Casey Jessup. She was my roommate."

Tony choked and bunched up the towel in his fist. Whatever he'd been expecting from them—that was not it.

"You're Martha?"

Martha's heart fluttered in her chest. "Yes. Casey mentioned me?"

"Uh-huh." He swept his head from side to

side, and then he focused on Cam. "Who's he? The po-po?"

"I'm not the police. I'm Martha's friend."

Cam narrowed his eyes. "Why are you worried about the police?"

"They don't know about me, do they?"

Martha shrugged. "Not that I know of. I didn't tell them anything about you. Why do you care? Shouldn't one of Casey's friends want to talk to the police about her suicide?"

"Friend? Yeah, I guess we were friends. I told her." He stopped and shook his head.

"Told her what? If you two weren't friends, how did you know her?"

"You really don't know, do you?"

"If I knew, I wouldn't be asking you."

"Casey was a paid girlfriend. You know, an escort."

Chapter Nine

She gaped at him like an idiot and then snapped her jaw closed.

Folding his hands around his glass, Cam leaned in. “She wasn’t an intern for some congresswoman?”

“Oh, yeah. She was all that, but she made the big money working as an escort—a professional girlfriend.” Tony cranked his head to the side to take in two men in suits talking at the end of the bar. “And I was her facilitator.”

“Her pimp, you mean.” Cam’s voice had roughened around the edges.

“That’s a harsh word for what I did. This is an upscale place, and when I ran into someone who was looking for that special girl, I referred that person to Casey. Sure, I got a cut of the action, but Casey was her own boss. She’d tried working for an agency, didn’t like it and struck out on her own. She just felt safe having me on her side, and man—" Tony wiped the corner of his eye with his towel "—I loved that girl."

"Tony!" The other bartender called out to her coworker and then held up one hand. "Never mind. You can take a break. It's slowing down."

"Do you want to join us at a table?" Cam jerked his thumb over his shoulder. "We have a few more questions for you, if you don't mind."

"I don't mind. Better you than the police. God, I hope they don't get suspicious about the suicide story and start digging into Casey's finances."

"Suicide *story*?" Cam lifted one eyebrow.

"C'mon. We all know it was murder. That's why you're here, isn't it?"

Martha's eyes met Cam's as Tony tossed his towel on the edge of the sink. He met them on the other side of the bar, and they crowded around a small cocktail table.

"Before we get started, I want you to know why we're here." Martha dragged the slip of paper with Casey's handwriting from her purse and flattened it in front of Tony. "Casey left this for me where we kept our extra key."

Tony smoothed his thumb over the words. "Inside the chair cover."

"She told you about that?"

"Casey told me everything." He picked up

the note and pressed his lips against the paper. "That's why she left this for you."

Having left his beer on the bar, Cam took a sip of Martha's club soda. "Start from the beginning. Are you the one who set her up with Congressman Wentworth?"

"I am, but the setup was a setup." Tony's gaze darted around the room, and he rubbed his upper lip. "Some guy who already knew about Casey's line of work approached me. Wentworth had been in here a few times—they all make it to this bar eventually."

"This guy wanted you to make sure Casey and Wentworth hooked up?" Martha crossed one leg over the other and kicked her foot back and forth.

"Exactly."

"He targeted Casey, didn't he? This man wanted Casey and only Casey for Wentworth. He already knew about her, knew she was an escort…knew she lived with Martha."

Cam's intensity had Tony shrinking back. "Y-yeah. It was all about reaching out to Casey and getting her to spy on her roommate, but Wentworth was definitely part of the equation, too. It had to be Wentworth for some reason."

Martha rubbed the goose bumps forming on her forearms. "It was a plan to get to me."

"I'm sorry. It was." Tony scratched the scruff

on his lean jaw. "But I don't know the details about that, and neither did Casey. He instructed her to steal your computer password, stuff like that."

"That's how he hacked into my laptop, how he took over my camera." She smacked her hand on the table, and her ice tinkled in protest.

"Look, Casey never got the impression this guy wanted to hurt you…or her. She wouldn't have done it, otherwise."

"Did she have a choice?" Cam's jaw formed a hard line. "Did he threaten to expose her? Expose her lifestyle? Yours?"

"Maybe there was a little of that, but no way would Casey, or me, be down with violence."

Martha folded the four corners of her cocktail napkin. "What about Wentworth? What was the plan with him?"

"Information. He wanted information from Wentworth." Tony chewed on the edge of his thumb. "The night Wentworth died at your place? Casey had been ordered to bring him back there that night once he started feeling sick. Usually they went to the apartment he kept in town. Casey had access to all his stuff there."

Cam tapped her thigh. "The emails, intel about Denver."

Tony looked from Cam to Martha, a deep crease between his eyebrows.

"Once he started feeling sick?" Martha ran her tongue around her dry mouth. "Did Casey do something to make Wentworth sick?"

"She didn't. No! She wouldn't do that." Tony dug his fingers into his spiky black hair, making it stand on end even more. "But she thinks someone slipped him something because her contact knew Wentworth would become ill that night and she had those orders to bring him back to her place when he did."

"So he'd die in my town house."

"Casey never thought that would be the endgame. She thought it was just a little information, some spy game that wouldn't affect anyone."

"Spy games always affect someone…including the spy." A dangerous light sparked in Cam's eyes. "Now you're going to tell us about this guy. What does he look like? What does he call himself? How does he contact you? Has he been in touch since Casey's murder?"

Tony spread his hands out on the table, his thumbs touching. "He introduced himself as Ben, but I'm sure we can all agree that's bogus. He's average, average everything except his beard. He wears a bushy beard and glasses.

Without that stuff, I probably wouldn't recognize him on the street."

Martha glanced at Cam. "Disguise."

"Yeah, probably." Tony rubbed his brow. "Always wore a hat, too. He comes in here when he wants to make contact."

Martha asked, "Does Ben show up at the bar when he wants to communicate with Casey or just you?"

"Both. He told her to get a temporary phone. They exchange messages that way."

Cam's eyebrows collided over his nose. "Did the cops mention anything to you about Casey having two phones, Martha?"

"No, and I had no idea she had two phones."

"If Ben was in that hotel room with Casey, I'm sure he took the burner phone with him when he left." Tony pinched the bridge of his nose, squeezing his eyes closed. "I can't believe she's gone."

"Why would Ben do it? Why kill Wentworth and Casey unless he got all he wanted from them and decided to tie up loose ends?" Cam drummed his fingers on the table.

"He had gotten what he wanted from them, and everything would've been status quo until he found out I kept those emails." Martha's bottom lip quivered. "I'm the one who caused all of this."

"Emails?" Tony's eyes flew open.

Cam drew his finger across his throat. "Need to know basis. Martha, none of this is your fault. If Casey hadn't been so greedy, she wouldn't have set you up and involved you in all this. If Wentworth had been able to keep it in his pants, he never would've been targeted."

Tony twirled the earring in his lobe. "And let's not leave out Ben himself. What information *did* he have Casey get from Wentworth, and how did it relate to you? Casey told me you were CIA."

"Like I said—need to know, and you don't," Cam growled. "What kind of man is a pimp anyway?"

"Hey, man. It wasn't like that. I protected Casey. I loved her."

"Dude, that's not love."

"A-are you going to tell the cops any of this? I'll deny everything."

"We're not ready to do that yet. We have no proof, but I'm not ruling it out when we do. Don't you want to see Casey's killer brought to justice?"

"I do, but it'll sacrifice her reputation."

"And yours." Cam rolled his eyes at Martha.

"If you're not a cop—" Tony waved at his coworker behind the bar "—why do you care about Ben? Whatever damage he caused has been done."

"I wanna know who he is and who he works for. The damage he did had a huge impact on a friend of mine, someone I admire and look up to. I'm not gonna let that slide. I'm not gonna let him get away with it."

Martha tapped on the table. "I have an idea. Doesn't this bar have security cameras? Would it be possible for us to see Ben?"

"I suppose I can offer to close up on my own, and you can meet me back here at closing. I'd have to disable the cameras or erase the footage so nobody sees you coming back here."

"I can take care of the camera. What time?"

"We close up at two."

Cam tapped his phone. "Almost three hours."

"We can go back to my place for a few hours."

Tony glanced over his shoulder and held up one finger at the other bartender. "I'll let you in the back door. Now I gotta go back to work."

As Tony walked away, Cam slumped back in his chair. "What do you think?"

"I can't believe I was so naive I didn't figure out Casey's real profession." Martha scooped her hair back from her face. "Is everyone in this town scamming?"

"It seems like it."

"Maybe it *is* time to call in the police."

He snorted. "Right. If we do that, you'll have to admit you stole those emails, and then it won't be just the police, it'll be the FBI. Your family doesn't have a great track record with the Fibbies."

"If everyone didn't have something to hide, including me, maybe we could actually get to the bottom of this." She sighed and stirred the melting ice in her glass.

"Maybe it is over for you, Martha." He took her hand and traced over her knuckles with his fingertip. "Ben or the patriot or whatever else he calls himself knows you have the emails, but you already sent them up the chain of command. His work is done. He showed his power and reach by killing Wentworth and Casey, and figures you're not going to do any more investigating. You can leave it now."

"But you're not going to."

He grabbed his coat from the back of the chair. "Let's go to your place."

"I'm going to use this time to pack up Casey's things for her family. Maybe we'll find this phone…or something else."

With one last look at Tony behind the bar and a nod, they slipped outside. Cam took the wheel of her car again and drove back to her place.

As they pulled up to the front, Cam said,

"Let's not forget. Ben could've been in possession of Casey's house key since last night."

Martha glanced up at the glow from the front window. She'd left a lamp on in the living room, so the light didn't surprise her or make her nervous—but Cam's words did.

She peeled her tongue from the roof of her dry mouth. "What if someone's in there?"

"I have my gun." He patted the pocket of his jacket. "Let me go in first."

He parked the car and then led the way up the steps to her town house. After she unlocked the door, he eased it open with his foot. He swung his weapon in front of him and stepped inside.

"Stay back, Martha."

She ducked behind his solid frame, but peeked around his body and surveyed the empty room. She let out a slow breath as Cam crept forward.

He waved his hand behind him, so she hovered in the entryway while he continued farther into the room. He poked his head around the corner to check out the kitchen. "Nobody in here."

He threw open the door to the half bathroom and then checked the lock on the back door. Pointing the barrel of his gun at the ceiling, he said, "I'll take a look upstairs."

"I'm coming with you." She turned and locked the front door although if Ben had Casey's key, that wouldn't do much good.

"Just stay behind me."

Martha followed Cam up the stairs and stayed back as he checked the second bathroom. When he pushed open her bedroom door, she held her breath and then released it when nothing but the silence of the room greeted them.

Cam turned, putting his finger to his lips, and yanked open the door of the master bathroom connected to the room. He shook his head. *"Nada."*

She crossed the hall to Casey's room, but Cam beat her there and pulled her back.

"One more."

He turned the handle and bumped the door with his shoulder. The door swung open and Cam crouched, clutching his weapon in front of him.

Martha gasped and pulled back, flattening herself against the opposite wall. Her fingers clawed against the smooth surface and she squeezed her eyes closed, waiting for… whatever.

Cam swore. "He was here. The bastard was here."

Martha peeled herself from the wall and

stumbled forward. Hanging on to the doorjamb, she leaned into Casey's bedroom and a chill zigzagged up her spine.

Someone had torn apart Casey's room looking for something, and Martha hoped to God he'd found it because if he hadn't, she had a feeling he'd come after her next.

CAM SHOVED HIS gun into the waistband of his pants. Whoever was responsible for tossing Casey's room had come and gone. He turned in a slow circle, surveying the damage. "What the hell is he looking for?"

"I don't know." Martha gulped in a breath and hiccupped. "But I hope he found it."

"You do?" Came drew his brows together. "I don't."

"Easy for you to say. It's not your place he's searching."

Cam smacked his fist into his palm. "You should've had your locks changed as soon as the police told you Casey's keys were missing. It's too late now."

Chewing on her bottom lip, Martha picked up one of Casey's T-shirts with two fingers and dropped it on the bed. "That's an understatement."

"I mean time-wise it's too late. You'll never get a locksmith out here at midnight."

"Luckily, I'm not staying here tonight. I'll get someone out first thing tomorrow morning." She ran her hands over a bunched-up pillow. "I'm sure as heck not going to work."

"What could Casey have that this guy wants?"

"And why didn't he ask her for it before he killed her?"

"Maybe he did and that's why he killed her. She wouldn't give it up."

Tilting her head to one side, Martha put a fist on her hip. "You met Casey. Tony told you what she did. Do you really think she's the kind of person who would die for her country? I'm pretty sure Casey would've given Ben whatever he wanted, especially if she thought it would save her life."

"You knew her better than I did." Cam rubbed his chin. "If Ben didn't ask her nicely for what he wanted or even threaten her if she didn't give it up, why? What is he looking for now? He has the emails."

"That's what I don't get." Martha collapsed on the foot of Casey's disheveled bed. "Ben sent me those emails, knowing I'd send them up the chain of command, and I did. Those messages launched the investigation into Major Denver, which then caused him to go AWOL. Mission accomplished."

"Not quite." Cam leveled a finger at Martha. "Nobody was expecting you to hold on to the emails yourself."

"It shouldn't matter to him. The emails reached their intended target and did the intended damage. So what if I have the emails on an external storage device? The only thing that does is open me up to charges within the Agency."

"It also proves you're suspicious about the emails. You said your superiors didn't take your concerns seriously or at least felt they'd done their due diligence in investigating them. For old Ben, case closed—until you messed things up. He tried warning you. He tried tying up his loose ends by killing both Wentworth and Casey."

"As far as he knows, those actions worked. I'm so terrified, I left my home. Why would he think I'd pursue it further?"

"Maybe he believes case is closed on you, too, but now he has another problem. Casey."

"And whatever evidence she left behind, perhaps linking Ben to the emails."

"He should be worried." Cam joined Martha on the bed. "Because if we find that evidence before he does, we might have some proof that the emails were all a scam."

"Maybe we don't need the evidence if we can ID the guy tonight on the bar's security video."

Cam pushed off the bed and spread his arms wide. "You wanted to start packing up Casey's things for her family. Now you have the incentive. I'll help you clean up this mess."

"Thanks. I'll get some garbage bags in case there isn't enough room in her suitcase for her clothes." Martha headed for the door and stopped. "Ben would've expected Casey to have the burner phone on her, wouldn't he?"

"Probably, if that's the way he contacted her."

"I mean, Tony told us she had a burner phone, but the cop didn't say anything to me about two phones. He mentioned her purse, her wallet and her cell phone. Wouldn't he have said two phones or maybe even asked me about two phones?"

Cam dragged a suitcase from the closet, which had also been thoroughly ransacked. "So, Ben took it, or that's what he's looking for."

"Maybe he found it in here, and now he'll leave me alone."

"If he did, that's one less thread of proof for us to tie him to Casey and the planting of the emails."

"C-can you blame me for wanting to back out of this mess? I know. I started out so full of myself, and now I'm just a coward."

"I wouldn't blame you at all, and you're far from a coward." He flipped open the suitcase. "Let's see what we can find out tonight, and if the video doesn't show us anything, you can call it a night…and forget the whole thing."

She dipped her chin to her chest and pivoted out of the room.

Cam started shoveling the clothes strewn about the room into the open suitcase. At least he had the emails. Martha would turn them over to him, and he could get someone else to look at them. Maybe he could convince someone in intelligence to look at the emails—if there were a way to leave Martha's name out of it.

Then his leave would be over, and he'd get sent on his next Delta deployment, and Martha could get back to doing what she did best—translating and following CIA rules. And their paths would never cross again.

His heart did a strange twist, and he thumped his fist against his chest.

"Playing Tarzan?" Martha leaned against the doorjamb, a garbage bag clutched in each hand.

"Just trying to clear my lungs. Dust." He

gestured to the suitcase, half-full with jumbled clothes. "Should I be folding up this stuff neatly?"

"I'll tell you what. You take a bag and fill it with the stuff from this desk." She thrust a plastic bag at him. "I'll pack her clothes."

They worked side by side, the silence broken by the occasional theory or rhetorical question.

Cam thumbed through Casey's papers before tossing them in the bag, but didn't find anything suspicious or out of the ordinary. He looked up when he'd cleared out the desk. "So, I guess professional girlfriends don't keep receipts or records. I've never even heard that term before. Where I come from, we have another name for it."

"I can't believe how naive I am." She dropped the lid on the suitcase and flattened one hand on the top while she zipped it. "I honestly just thought Casey had a lot of boyfriends and dates."

"How were you supposed to know? She hardly fits the profile of a hooker."

Martha raised one finger. "Professional girlfriend, and I guess she *is* the profile."

Cam slid his phone from his pocket and glanced at the time. "It's almost two. We should be heading back to the bar. I hope Tony has something to show us."

Martha followed Cam out of Casey's room and stopped at the door, turning around to look at their handiwork. "Her family hasn't even contacted me to pick up Casey's things. Maybe that's why she did it, the girlfriend thing."

"Why?"

"She just wanted some love, even if it was pretend."

BY THE TIME they got back to the Insider, the traffic on the street had thinned out but not disappeared. Martha parked on a side street, and they slipped into the alley behind the bar.

They reached the door, and Cam pointed to a wedge jammed beneath the bottom of the door to prop it open.

Martha tipped her head back and tugged on Cam's sleeve. "Looks like he already disabled the camera."

Cam looked up and his brow creased. "He sprayed the lens. I guess that way it doesn't look like the camera has been tampered with, as long as it cleans off."

"We'll have to remind him to wipe it off."

Cam used his foot to push open the door, and Martha stepped inside the back hallway of the bar.

She whispered Tony's name.

"He's probably in the office." Cam nudged

her back, and she veered toward a closed door past the restrooms.

"Tony?" She knocked, pressing her ear against the door.

Cam stepped around her and opened the door, pushing it wide.

The computer on the desk glowed, and Cam hunched over it. "Looks like he's already been checking the security camera footage."

Martha backed up a step, one arm wrapped around her midsection. "Where is he? He should've heard us come in by now."

Cam reached into his pocket and Martha's heart skipped a beat, knowing that's where he'd stashed his gun.

Cam waved her away from the door and he crept through it, squeezing past her.

She followed him down the hallway to the bar…and then wished she hadn't.

Tony was still here all right—slumped at a table, his head resting in a pool of blood.

Chapter Ten

The floorboards creaked behind him, and Cam whipped around from Tony's dead body, clutching his weapon.

Martha gaped back at him, her face white and her mouth wide.

"Get back. He's dead."

"What happened to him?"

Cam launched forward and ran down the hallway toward the back door, which they'd left propped open. He pulled it closed and locked it.

When he returned to the bar, Martha was leaning over Tony, both hands over her mouth. If she got sick all over the body, they'd have more explaining to do than he was prepared for.

"Martha, what are you doing?"

"He left us a message."

"Tony?" He joined her at the table and then

jerked back. Someone had written on the table in Tony's blood: "Back off."

Martha stumbled back from the table, as if obeying the order written on it. "That's for us. He knew. He knew about this meeting, or suspected it and was watching Tony."

Cam backtracked to the mahogany bar and peered over it at the register, gaping open. "He staged this as a burglary. Cleaned out the cash. He took care of the security cameras, too."

"And probably deleted the rest of the footage showing his meetings with Tony."

"We're done here." Cam leaned over the bar and grabbed a clean bar towel. "Did you touch anything at the table?"

"God, no." She shoved her hands in her pockets.

"Then we need to clean off our prints in the office—on the door and the computer keyboard—and at the back door. At least our images won't be on security footage, either."

As he made for the office, Martha grabbed his back pocket. "You mean we're going to just leave him here without calling the police?"

He glanced over his shoulder at her. "And how would that story go? We came here after hours to meet with Tony and get a look at security footage of his meeting with a man who knows you stole classified emails from your employer—the CIA?"

She sagged against the wall outside the office. "That's the problem with lying, isn't it? It never stops. You have to tell more and more lies to cover up the previous lies."

"I'd lie to hell and back to protect you, Martha. You don't need to get in trouble for something you did that felt right at the time."

"I guess that's what my father would've said. It felt right at the time. Your father, too."

He ran the towel across the computer's keyboard. "What we're doing doesn't compare to what our fathers did. Not even close. You sensed something was off about those emails—and you were right—but nobody believed you. You just took matters into your own hands."

"And made a mess of things."

Cam wiped down the front of the door and then, with the towel in his hand, closed it and finished off with the doorknob. "By keeping those emails, you forced Ben out into the open. He's running scared. If you hadn't stored those messages on a flash drive, Ben would've been home free."

"He might not have killed Wentworth, Casey and Tony though."

"Really?" Cam got to work on the back

door, deleting their after-hours visit. "I think he would have. He didn't want to leave any witnesses."

"So we just leave Tony like this?"

"Nothing we can do for him now. He was playing with fire, and he knew it."

She tipped her head down the hallway. "What about the message on the table? Should we wipe that off?"

"Let the cops puzzle it out. If we wipe it up, the police are going to be able to tell something was there. Why would a killer wipe up his victim's blood?"

Cam shoved the block of wood beneath the door with his foot to prop it open again, leaving everything as they'd found it when they arrived. "Now we just have to hope nobody saw us go in here."

"I was watching." Martha pulled her keys from her purse. "Nobody saw us."

They slipped into the alley, and Cam did a quick survey of the surrounding businesses. "I'm pretty sure Tony's killer took care of the other cameras in this alley that would have a shot at the Insider's back door."

"He's protecting us at the same time he's protecting himself." Martha sidled along the back wall of the building for good measure.

When they got to the street with the car,

they ducked inside, just a couple of late-night bar-hoppers along with other stragglers on the sidewalk "This is going to be all over the news tomorrow. Do you think the police will make the connection between Casey and Tony?"

"They're going to look at him more closely because of that message, but I don't know why they'd connect him to Casey. As far as the cops are concerned, Casey's death is a suicide and they don't seem to be going through her contacts." Martha put the car in gear and eased away from the curb.

"They might be going through the contacts of her burner phone—if they had it."

She pulled around the corner, checking the rearview mirror. "And you're thinking if Ben had that phone, he wouldn't be running around murdering people and sending me warnings?"

"Oh, he still would've murdered Tony because he had access to that footage showing Ben meeting with him and Casey in the Insider."

"He obviously didn't think that footage was important enough to kill for—until we showed up. He must be following us. He knew we'd paid a visit to Tony."

"He could've been watching Tony. Where are you going?"

"To drop you off at your hotel."

"If you think I'm letting you go back to your mother's place alone tonight, you're crazy. I'm camping out on that ritzy sofa in the living room."

Cam could just make out the pink tint to Martha's cheek. She wanted him there. Maybe she even wanted *him*.

"Okay. Th-that actually makes me feel better, safer. If he thinks I have something he wants, who knows what lengths he's willing to go to get it?"

"And if it's that phone, it could blow his cover if Casey has texts with him on there."

"If his phone is a temp, too, how is Casey's phone going to incriminate him?"

"There could be ways to track those phones. Just the fact that Casey might have texts giving her instructions on what to do about Wentworth would be huge, especially if those instructions mention Denver and our assignments."

Her hand slid from the steering wheel and dropped to his thigh. "That might not be enough to clear his name. There's more evidence against him than what was uncovered as a result of those damned messages."

"I know that, but it's a start. If bogus, planted emails initiated the entire investigation, it'll cast suspicions over the rest of the so-called evidence."

"You'll never give it up, will you? Major Denver means that much to you?"

"Everything." Cam closed his eyes as a sharp pain pierced his gut.

The pressure of Martha's hand on his leg soothed his hurt and frustration.

"I understand." Her whispered words floated toward him. "When my father first came under investigation, I believed with all my heart that he was innocent. I was willing to do anything to prove it. I think that's why he finally admitted his guilt."

"Why?"

"He couldn't stand to see my vehemence in his defense when he knew it was all a lie."

Her voice broke, and he covered her hand with his—the soothed become the soother.

"He loved you though, despite his shortcomings." He traced the tips of her fingers, outlining her hand. "And you love him, despite your disappointment in him."

She sniffled. "I tried to hate him, but I didn't have it in me."

"He made a big, big mistake and he's paying for it. Don't charge him an even bigger price by withdrawing your love from him."

Her head jerked toward him and then back

to the road. "You wouldn't be so forgiving of your father, would you?"

"Two different situations." He rubbed a circle in the condensation on the window with his fist. "Your father did what he did out of greed. Sure, he wasn't thinking of the consequences to his family, but he never stopped loving or caring for that family. My father didn't give a damn about my mother or me and my sister."

"I guess." She slid her hand from beneath his and wrapped her fingers around the steering wheel. "Totally different situation between my father and Major Denver, too. You're convinced he's innocent."

"Absolutely." He smacked a hand against his thigh. "He's being set up, and we're going to figure out by who and why."

"We?"

"The rest of our Delta Force team. Most of us don't believe the charges against him, and we've made a pact to clear his name."

"Then I'm glad to be part of that. If my father isn't deserving of my efforts, I believe you when you say Major Denver is."

They drove the rest of the way back to Martha's mother's house in silence, his thoughts on his good-for-nothing father and hers probably on her own father—two men who couldn't be more dissimilar, from two different sides of the tracks, but who'd both made bad choices that ultimately hurt their families.

If he ever got the opportunity to be a father, he'd do things differently, but he'd need a partner who could tame him. He slid a sidelong glance at Martha's profile, her pert nose and wide mouth, giving her a look of innocence. Maybe her sweet expression gave people the impression they could take advantage of her.

She pulled into her mother's driveway and cut the engine. "We should've stopped by your hotel so you could pick up some of your things. My mom has plenty of extra toothbrushes and toiletries, but I'm pretty sure you don't want to wear any of my dad's clothes now that orange is his new black."

"Probably not, but I'll take the toothbrush."

While she disarmed the alarm system and unlocked the door, Cam faced outward, his muscles tense. He'd made sure they weren't followed from the bar, but he'd bet Ben knew about Martha's mom's house out here on the bay.

Martha pushed open the door, and Cam followed her inside, close on her heels. She locked up from the inside and entered the alarm's code.

She tossed her purse and coat onto the nearest chair and covered her face with both hands.

"You okay?" Cam stroked her back, which arched slightly like a satisfied cat's.

"It's been a long, long day." Her hands moved from her face through the coffee-colored strands of her hair. "I can't believe we were so close to getting a look at Casey's contact and to have it all end in Tony's gruesome murder. I'd never seen a dead body before in my life, and I just chalked up three. How is that possible?"

"I know." He touched her arm. In fact, he couldn't seem to stop touching her. "I'm sorry you had to see any of it, but I'm glad you're still safe."

She turned wide eyes on him. "For how much longer? He's looking for something of Casey's, and he wants to find it before I do. If he doesn't, he may just be satisfied with making sure I never find it either, and the only way to do that is by making sure I meet the same fate as Wentworth, Casey and Tony."

"Do you think I'm gonna let that happen?" He gripped her shoulders.

"You do have a life, a job, outside of saving Major Denver." She dropped her gaze. "Saving me."

"Not yet. We have time. We're going to find what this guy's looking for, and we're going to implicate him. I'll be here for you, Martha."

Tipping her head to the side, she rubbed her cheek against the back of his hand. “Are you saving me because you can’t save him, Cam? Or is saving me mixed up in your mind with saving him?”

“What does that mean?” He stepped back. “Do you think you’re some sort of substitute for Denver?”

She raised her shoulders, rolling them at the same time, dislodging his hands. “If you could prove his innocence tomorrow in some other place, with someone else’s help, wouldn’t you?”

His brows shot up. “And leave you? Leave you in this situation without protection?”

Her chin began to dip, and he pinched it and tilted her head back.

“I want to help Denver. That’s why I came out here in the first place, but you’re my first priority now, Martha.”

A tear danced on the ends of her long lashes. “I don’t think I’ve ever been someone’s first priority before.”

His hand slid along her jaw, and he captured her earlobe between his fingers. “I may not be the brightest guy in the world, but I know a precious gem when I see it.”

She blinked, dislodging the tear, which splashed on the back of his hand. “Some of the brightest guys in the world don't have kind hearts like yours."

The side of his mouth twitched into a half smile. "I've never heard that one before."

Crossing one hand over the other, she pressed them against his chest. "That's because you've never bothered to let anyone in before. Too busy being the big, macho lug."

His heart thundered under the pressure of her hands, and he expanded his chest. "You found me out."

She looked around, as if aware of her surroundings for the first time. "Why are we still standing here in the entryway? It's almost dawn."

"Good thing neither of us has a job to go to." A slow pulse beat in his throat as he looked down into Martha's face. He just needed some sign from her. Anything they did had to originate from her desire. He had to avoid even a hint of coercion or persuasion.

Her gaze meandered to his mouth, as her own lips parted and her fingertips curled into the material of his shirt.

He brushed a kiss across her forehead, and she sighed, dropping her shoulders. His next kiss landed on her cheekbone.

This time she shifted from one foot to the

other, moving closer so that the tips of her breasts made contact with his chest.

He swallowed. “Do you want to sit down?”

She rested her forehead on his collarbone. “I want to go to bed—with you.”

Her simple request lit a fire in his belly, and he pulled her against his body, wrapping his arms around her waist and resting his cheek against the top of her head.

“I want that, too.” As he spoke, the stubble on his chin caught the wavy strands of her hair. This slow burn between them made him harder than if she’d ripped his clothes off.

“Shouldn’t we make a move upstairs?” She pulled away from him, but they were still connected through her wisps of hair that clung to his chin.

That’s how he felt with Martha—connected—as if she always had some hold on a part of him.

MARTHA’S STOMACH DROPPED. Cam didn’t really want her. He was being polite…too damned polite. She turned away from him quickly and stumbled on the first step of the staircase, grabbing the bannister.

He caught her around the waist, more to steady her than make a move on her. “H-have you changed your mind?”

"No, but I think you have." She broke away from him and charged up the stairs.

His footsteps pounded behind her. She felt the air at her back as he made a swipe at her blouse, and she took the next set of steps two at a time.

"Martha, wait." This time he grabbed her swinging arm and pulled her down one step. "What did I do wrong?"

Her whiskey eyes flashed at him. "I just told you I wanted to go to bed with you. Maybe it was clumsy or whatever. Maybe I should've batted my lashes and swiveled my nonexistent hips, but I thought it was pretty direct."

A slow flush crawled up his neck. "And I thought my answer was direct. It's what I want, too."

"But then you—' she wrinkled her nose "—you hugged me, put your cheek on my hair. Comforted me."

"So." He spread his hands and hunched his shoulders. "What does that mean? We just came from a murder scene. I figured you needed some comfort."

She bit her bottom lip. What did it mean? It had felt...brotherly. She was done being everyone's favorite little sister.

"It's just not the reaction I expected after telling you I wanted to sleep with you."

"What did you expect?" Cam leaned against the bannister as if waiting for a long, drawn-out explanation.

"I expected you to j-jump my bones. Rip my clothes off." A hurt little bark escaped from her throat. "I guess I just don't inspire that kind of passion."

A slow smile crept across his mouth, and before she had time to ask him what it meant, he had her against the wall, pressing the full length of his body against hers.

He captured her wrists in one hand, dragged her arms above her head and pinned them to the wall. He growled, his lips one hot breath away from hers. "You talk too much."

The kiss he planted on her mouth heated her blood. Her knees wobbled. Her skin tingled. Her lashes fluttered closed and as his tongue invaded her mouth, she wrapped one leg around his in an attempt to stay upright.

When he finished draining her with that one kiss, he unbuttoned her pants. To allow him to pull them down easily, she arched her back. Instead, with her pants still around her hips, Cam plunged his hand inside her panties, and she gasped at the sweet invasion.

He toyed with the swollen folds of her flesh, and she closed around his fingers as she rocked against him.

She couldn't just let him do all the work, but his other hand still held her wrists captive. She rested her head on his shoulder and pressed her lips against his neck.

As she got closer to her release, she bared her teeth against his skin and nipped at it.

And then it happened. Her orgasm clawed through her body, and her head fell back against the wall, banging it.

Cam tucked his hand beneath her bottom, his fingers still toying with her, as she rocked against him.

He released her wrists, and she grabbed the front of his shirt. With shaking fingers she unbuttoned it, fanned it out and slipped it from his arms.

His broad chest looked chiseled from granite. With a fever burning in her veins, she trailed her fingers from his throat to the waistband of his jeans

As she worked on the fly, Cam braced his hands against the wall on either side of her and kept dipping his head to tease her with kisses.

"I thought you were supposed to be ripping my clothes off. You're kinda slow."

She yanked his fly open and skimmed her palm over the bulge in his briefs. "Oh, I want you."

He toed off his shoes and kicked them down

the stairs. Then he shed his jeans and his underwear at the same time and kicked them off the side of the staircase.

He tugged at her clothing, not quite ripping it off, and dropped each piece over the bannister to the floor below to join his clothes.

For a brief moment she thought he'd taken her hand to lead her up the rest of the staircase to her bedroom. Instead, he urged her down to the step directly beneath her.

She sat with her legs extended down the stairs, as he crouched beside her. Looked like she'd have to wait to have him because he seemed intent on having her again.

He spread her legs, and the toes of her left foot curled around the wooden balusters that drilled into each step. He positioned himself between her thighs a few steps below her.

When his tongue touched her aching flesh, her bottom bounced from the step.

"You're not going anywhere." He flattened his palms against her inner thighs and dipped his head to renew his tender assault.

She didn't even last as long as the previous time, and the heat surged through her body and into her cheeks as her orgasm raced through every cell of her body.

He came up for air and rested his chin on her mound as she still writhed beneath him.

"That didn't take long. Either you haven't had sex in a while, or I'm the greatest lover known to womankind."

"It's been years."

Cam's eyes popped open, and Martha giggled as she ran one foot up the back of his leg and planted it against his muscled buttocks. "I'm just kidding."

"You're cruel." He reached up and cupped one of her breasts. "And who knew Martha Drake giggled?"

"Only when she's with the greatest lover known to womankind."

He rose above her, as if doing a push-up over her body, and skimmed the tip of his erection along her belly. "I haven't even gotten started yet."

He grabbed the bannister and pulled himself up, hooking one arm around her waist. He pressed his naked body against hers and kissed her hard and long.

"Where the hell is your bedroom in this dump?"

She traced his perfect form with her hands on either side of his body and trailed her fingertips across his smooth, tight skin. "I thought you'd never ask."

"I could take you right here on the staircase if you want." He tapped the hard wood of the bannister. "Lean you right over and claim you from behind."

"But my bed is so soft and warm."

"Just like you." He swept her up in his arms, cradling her five-foot-ten-inch frame against his chest like she was a teddy bear.

Her head fell into the hollow of his shoulder, fitting perfectly, and her mouth watered as she anticipated the other perfect fit between their bodies.

She directed him to her bedroom, and he kicked open the half-closed door, which gave her a thrill. As he dropped her on the bed, she reached for him with greedy hands.

Grabbing those hands, he kissed her fingertips. "You're so beautiful. I watched your face during your first orgasm, and it was like witnessing the birth of a butterfly."

A wash of red immediately claimed Cam's cheeks. "Was that the stupidest comparison ever?"

A tear leaked out of the corner of her eye. "That was the sweetest thing anyone has ever said to me. The best bit of poetry I've ever heard."

"You're just saying that." He stretched out beside her and caressed every inch of her body as he rained kisses all over her face.

She wanted to pleasure him, too, but he wouldn't allow it

He whispered in her ear, "This is all about you tonight. I want you to feel pampered, desired..."

Loved. She wanted to feel loved, but what right did she have to expect that from Cam? She'd practically dragged him into bed. What was he going to do, turn her down? Cam Sutton was a hot-blooded, all-American male. Men like Cam didn't turn down invitations to sex—ever.

As he began moving against her, spreading her open, entering her, all her insecurities slipped away in breathless wanting. He filled her up, seemed to find every deficit in her soul and had an answer for it.

This time, she got to watch him as he experienced his release, and the sheer pleasure that spasmed across his face gave her a sense of power and tenderness at the same time. For several moments, she held his joy cupped within her.

As he shifted off her body, he nuzzled her neck. "I don't know if that just made the situation between us better or worse."

She froze, her fingers ceasing their combing his hair back from his forehead. "What does that mean? How can what we just experienced make anything worse? Unless I just misread everything that happened."

"You didn't misread a damned thing, Martha." He rolled to his side and propped up his head with his hand, his elbow digging into the pillow. "That was incredible and we both know it, but I still have to protect you. I don't know how I can do that job with a clear head now."

"It'll be better." She traced his bottom lip with her thumb. "Now that we've gotten the sex part out of the way, we'll be able to focus better on the issues in front of us."

His eyebrows shot up. "The sex part?"

"You know, all that tension between us, or at least on my side?" She tried to keep the insecure questioning out of her voice but failed miserably.

"I know exactly what you mean." He kissed the pad of her thumb.

She cupped his jaw briefly with her hand. "I'm going to pick up our clothes downstairs."

He grabbed her hand as she rolled from the bed. "I can do that if it's driving you crazy knowing they're in heaps on the floor."

"That's okay. I'm going to get some water, too."

Yawning, he settled back against the pillow. "Hurry back."

From the edge of the bed, she surveyed his

heavy lids and slow, steady breathing. She rolled her eyes. Even if she hurried, he'd probably be sleeping by the time she came back.

She tiptoed from the room and crept down the stairs, picking up items of clothing as she went. She gathered up the rest of their things where Cam had dropped them over the bannister, and her lips twitched. He'd really shown her a night of passion.

She bundled the clothes on a chair and flicked on the lights beneath the kitchen cabinets. She grabbed a glass from the cupboard and turned toward the fridge.

A quick movement caught her eye, and she glanced at the sliding glass doors to the back. She let out a scream and dropped the glass on the floor where it shattered.

But she still couldn't tear her gaze away from a pair of gleaming eyes that had caught her in their malevolent stare.

Chapter Eleven

A crash and a scream from Martha yanked Cam to full consciousness. He bolted upright and reached for his gun…which he'd left downstairs in his jacket.

"Martha!" Scrambling from the bed, he scanned the floor for his briefs and remembered he'd dropped them over the stairs. "Just great."

He stumbled for the door and charged down the stairs, calling Martha's name again. He followed the glow of the low light emanating from the kitchen.

He almost plowed into Martha's back as he launched into the kitchen.

She stumbled forward, and he caught her around the waist as she raised her arm, pointing toward the sliding door to the back of the house.

He peered at the darkness beyond the glass, beyond the reflection of the two of them naked and entwined in some other kind of dance from the one they'd left upstairs. Martha's body was stiff and unyielding, and she hadn't said one word to him since that scream had echoed throughout the house.

Giving her a little shake, he asked, "What's wrong? What happened, Martha? Did you see something outside?"

She cranked her head to the side and worked her mouth for a few seconds before she finally found her voice. "A man. A man with a black ski mask covering his whole face was looking in at me."

Adrenaline ripped through Cam's body and he lunged for the door, but Martha grabbed his arm.

"Wait. There's glass on the floor and…and you don't have any clothes on."

"More importantly, I don't have my weapon." He spun around and strode to the chair where he'd left his jacket. He plunged his hand in the pocket and grabbed his gun. He swiped his jeans from the same chair and struggled into them on his way back to the kitchen.

This time he nearly tripped over Martha, on her hands and knees, sweeping a towel across the kitchen floor.

"You need shoes. I think I pushed most of the glass aside, but it's freezing out there.

Your shoes are under the chair where I put our clothes."

With the intruder most likely putting more and more distance between himself and the house—and Cam's gun—Cam turned and stuffed his bare feet into his shoes. Finally, he charged outside.

Martha had turned on the outdoor lights, and Cam scanned the small patio and the lawn beyond it, which tumbled down to the boat dock and the bay. He took the corner of the house and ran in a crouched position to the front.

He peered around the corner to the driveway, but if the masked man had arrived in a car and driven up to the front of the house, he was gone now. It made sense that Ben would know about this place. He seemed to know everything else about Martha.

The cold night air seeped into his bare flesh as he made his way to the circular driveway. He cocked his head, listening for—anything, a receding car, the squeal of a tire. He heard nothing but his own heart slamming against his chest.

He returned to the back patio where Martha hovered at the sliding door, his jacket clasped to her chest.

"Nothing out front?"

"No."

She thrust the jacket at him when he got close. "Put this on. It's freezing out here."

Poking his arms through the sleeves, he asked, "What was he doing at the door? What did you see?"

"Not much." She hugged herself. "I glanced up and saw his face at the door, except it wasn't really his face. His face was completely covered by a ski mask."

"Did he try to get in?"

"I-I'm not sure. He didn't run away until you got down here."

"Close the door. I want to check something."

Martha stepped onto the patio next to him and slid the door closed.

Cam ran his hand over the window closest to the door handle, skimming his palm over the chilly glass. Then he felt it. His fingertips traced over a rough edge in the glass.

"Did you find anything?"

"I did. Feel this." He took her hand and guided her fingers over the damaged window.

She snatched her hand back and wrinkled her nose. "It's cut."

"He used some glass-cutting tool. He was going to slice out a part of the window and reach in to unlock the door."

She jerked upright. "He knows about this house."

"Of course he does, Martha."

Flicking her fingers at the window, she jerked

upright. "That's what he was doing when I discovered him. He stopped because you came onto the scene. I guess he wasn't expecting anyone else to be here."

"Too bad I wasn't prepared for him." He snapped his fingers. "The camera system. I noticed the house has cameras on all corners. Can you pull that up on the computer?"

"Yes." She sighed. "The sun's going to be coming up soon anyway. Who needs sleep?"

He caught a strand of her hair and wrapped it around his finger. "I'd rather do what we did instead of sleep any day of the week."

"Me, too."

He tugged her forward by her hair and kissed her sweet lips. "Video."

"Maybe you could put on the rest of your clothes, so I won't get distracted." She wiggled her fingers in the air over his bare chest, and his skin tingled as if she'd actually touched him.

"Yeah, distractions." He yanked open the sliding glass door and stalked to the chair where a lone shirt hung. Martha had already put on all her clothes from last night.

At the entrance to a door off the main hallway, Martha crooked her finger at him. "The office. My mom's desktop computer is in here, and we can look up the footage."

Martha stationed herself behind the big desk and clicked on a lamp. “Let me see if I can remember how to retrieve it.”

“It’s all pretty standard.” He leaned over her shoulder as she clicked through the files on the computer’s desktop.

The monitor displayed four squares, and Martha poked at each one as she identified it. “Driveway, front door and porch, back door, boat dock.”

“Time?” He swirled his finger around the date and time stamp in the lower-right corner of each panel.

Martha enlarged the driveway display and moved the cursor to the menu. She adjusted the time to just about thirty minutes before she went downstairs.

Cam squinted at the video. “Is it motion-activated?”

“I honestly don’t know that much about it, but I think so. It’s just dark, isn’t it?”

“Do you know for sure if it works?”

She slumped against the deep, leather chair. “No.”

“Maybe he didn’t come up the driveway. He wouldn’t be that obvious, would he? I didn’t see or hear any evidence that he had a car out front. Switch to another view. We know for sure he was at the back door.”

Martha switched to the video panel showing the back door and made it bigger. She set the time back, and they both stared at the murky display again.

The image came to life and Cam let out a breath. "There he is."

A figure moved into the frame, a ski mask pulled low over his face, dark, baggy clothing loose around his body.

Martha bolted upright. "That's our guy."

"Unfortunately, that could be any guy. That could be me or even you. Just like using a disguise at the Insider, he's covering up."

The man came in from the side and crowded the door for several seconds, hunching over.

"He's probably working on the window."

The man stood still, placing gloved hands against the door, staring into the house.

"Ugh, that's probably when I noticed him."

The intruder sprang back from the door, stumbling over a potted plant. He dashed toward the lawn and out of the camera's view.

"He's heading toward the boat dock." Martha pulled up that panel, but the camera recorded nothing, no movement at all. "That one might be broken."

"We wouldn't have been able to identify him anyway, not with that ski mask."

Martha shoved back from the desk. "I wish

I knew what he wanted. He must've come here to break in and do a search."

"If all he wanted to do was search your place for whatever he thinks Casey left you, he would've taken off when you appeared in the kitchen and caught him red-handed."

Slowly turning the chair to face him, Martha asked, "Do you think he wanted to harm me this time?"

"You said he didn't leave until I stumbled onto the scene. You'd already noticed him, and that didn't make him go away."

"So, he's reached the point where he doesn't want to take a chance that I'll discover his identity from something Casey might have left behind." Martha's fingers clawed into the arms of the chair.

Cam bent forward and smoothed his hands down her arms. "Maybe he just wanted to question you."

"Question?" She tilted her head back to meet his eyes. "Is that a nice way of saying interrogate under a single bright light? The man's a killer, Cam. He's proven that three times now."

"He *is* desperate to protect his identity. He probably never figured you'd find Tony and never figured Tony would fess up to being Casey's pimp."

"But I did, and Tony did and now we have

a chance to discover who this guy is and why he set me up with those emails about Major Denver."

"And who's giving him orders." Cam's jaw tightened. "I'd like to get *him* under a single bright light to find that out."

"He must know we don't have this super-secret thing he's searching for because he's still after it—and us. I don't understand why he doesn't just disappear." She cupped his jaw with her hand. "Even if we get a good look at him and we're able to convince the FBI or the CIA to investigate him for those emails, it's not going to change anything for Denver, is it? There's still the rest of the evidence against the major that these emails brought to light."

"It's a start. It's a connection. Right now, we don't know who set him up or why. If this Ben can give us some insight, maybe we can unravel the rest of it."

"Then it's a game of cat and mouse, isn't it? We try to find the evidence, and he tries to make sure we don't. When is he going to give it up?"

Cam shrugged and pulled her out of the chair. "When he's tired of playing cat and mouse."

"Or when I'm dead."

"Don't say that." He placed his hands on her shoulders and drove his thumbs into her skin.

"We both know the reason why he hasn't taken his shot at me yet."

"We do?" Cam ran his tongue over his dry lips.

"It's because you're here, Cam. He knows I have some kind of badass bodyguard dogging me, and when you leave—" her shoulders tensed beneath his hands "—I'm a goner."

"I'm not going anywhere."

"Yet." She tucked her head beneath his chin. "How many more days until you leave?"

"Shh." He dropped his hands to her waist and pulled her body against his. "We have time. I'm gonna catch this guy and when I do, he'll pay—for everything."

LATER THAT MORNING, Martha, still sleepy-eyed, greeted him in the kitchen, holding up a plate of eggs. "Scrambled. Is that okay with you?"

"You didn't have to make breakfast…but I'm glad you did." He straddled the stool at the island counter. "I'd like to have a look out back now that it's light and see if Ben left anything. Would also be interesting to figure out how he got here. Unless that camera out front is broken like the one at the boat dock, he didn't come up the driveway."

She dropped two slices of toast on his plate and put it on the place mat in front of him. "I wanted to show you the boat dock, anyway. It's not as big as the one we had when my dad was a free man, but it's similar."

"Must've been an idyllic childhood."

"It was lonely. I didn't make friends easily, and my mother insisted on sending me to a private school, miles away from our house. My parents' home wasn't exactly part of a neighborhood." She waved her fork around. "Kind of like this place. I couldn't run down the block to play with friends. That's one of the reasons why I read a lot—and hung out with my dad."

"At least you had a dad you could hang out with…and at least you could read." Cam shook his head as soon as the words left his lips. "I sound like a self-pitying idiot."

She smiled, and his world got brighter by several shades.

"A little, but it's safe to do that with me. At least you had godlike good looks and athletic abilities. You must've been Mr. Popularity growing up."

"Yeah, but that can get kind of lonely too in its own way."

She sat on the stool next to him and bumped his shoulder with hers. "Two lonely kids and now here we are."

"No place I'd rather be." He dabbed a crumb from the corner of her mouth. "When I discovered the identity of the CIA translator who turned over the emails that upended Denver's life, I was ready to give you the third degree. I thought you might've even been involved in the setup—until I met you. Then I knew exactly why you'd been the conduit for those emails."

"Because of my rigid adherence to protocol."

"But you surprised me, and you sure as hell surprised Ben."

She twirled her fork on her plate. "Do you think the patriot and Ben are the same person? We've been assuming they are, but maybe we're dealing with two different people—the computer geek and the killer."

"Could be." He brushed the toast crumbs from his fingers into the napkin on his lap. "The patriot warned you the night before Wentworth's death. That's for sure. He knew that was coming."

"Just seems like we're dealing with someone who has two very different sets of skills."

"A computer nerd can't be a killer? Or an assassin can't also be well versed in computer programming?"

"Anything's possible, but I dated a tech whiz and I couldn't see him taking out Tony like that."

So, Martha did date. Cam stirred the eggs around his plate, intently studying the pattern they made. "What happened to that relationship?"

"Bad idea all around. We were too much alike, and I worked with him or at least near him."

"CIA analyst?"

"Not nearly that exciting. CIA tech guy."

"Who broke it off?"

"I sort of did. It wasn't that serious to even be called a breakup. We talked a lot. We were friends first, and then he got the bright idea to ask me out. He never even saw the inside of my bedroom."

Cam raised his eyebrows. Was that Martha's way of telling him she hadn't slept with the guy? "Still friends?"

"We chat when we see each other at work." She picked up her plate and held it out toward him. "Are you done?"

He stacked his plate on top of hers. "That hit the spot. Now let's bundle up and take a look around outside."

Martha left their plates in the sink, and they grabbed their jackets. When they slipped through the back door that had been compromised the previous night, Cam stepped back and looked at the scratches on the window.

He rubbed the rough patch of glass. “You should get this fixed. It wouldn’t take much to punch that out. He was probably minutes away from doing that.”

“Add it to my list, which includes getting my Georgetown locks changed.”

Cam crouched and searched the ground in front of the door. The mat seemed undisturbed, and the brick beneath didn’t show any marks or footprints, not even theirs from last night.

He took two steps back, grazed the edge of the planter with his leg and squatted beside the container to study the plant for threads.

“You’re retracing his steps?” Martha tilted her head.

“Yeah. It looked like he ran straight back to the boat dock and the bay.”

Martha turned and faced the water. The brisk breeze blew her hair back from her face. “He must have, unless he circled back to the front, but we didn’t see anything on the camera footage. Maybe he came up by water.”

“You did want to show me the boat dock.”

She stuck her hand out behind her. “Let’s go.”

In two strides he joined her and grabbed her hand. Their footsteps crunched on the gravel path leading toward the dock.

Cam stopped and dropped to one knee. “If he took this path, he would’ve left footprints.”

Martha crouched beside him and poked at the gravel with her finger. “Looks like he may have even smoothed this over by shuffling his feet.”

“Maybe, or the wind covered his tracks.” Cam cupped her elbow and helped her rise. “I think we’re on the right track here.”

When they reached the dock, Cam stomped on it. “Sturdier than it looks.”

“It has to hold up to the weather, especially this time of year.” She pounded on the side of the shed that was designed to hold a small boat. “This, too, even though my mom doesn’t have a boat.”

Cam peered around the corner at the water stirring inside the empty boat shed. “Maybe he parked his own boat here when he came up.”

Martha placed her hands on her hips and stared at the gray water lapping at the shore. “He could’ve come from the public dock, moored here and then attempted his break-in. When you showed up, he hightailed it back to his boat and took off, probably knowing you’d look for a car out front.”

“I probably could’ve caught him if I’d come straight back here instead of wasting time putting clothes on and going to the front of the house." He fired a pebble into the water.

"You couldn't have come out here without your clothes." Martha moseyed to the edge of the dock and kicked at the mooring.

"Don't fall in." Cam leaned over to gather a few more stones for skipping, and a half-smoked cigarette on the shore. He pinched it between his thumb and forefinger and held it up. "Look at this. Does your mother smoke?"

"No."

He cupped it in his palm and bounced it in his hand. "This looks hand rolled. Would anyone else be down here? It's dry. Looks like someone meant to toss it in the water and missed—maybe because it was dark."

"My mom's handyman smokes. He's married to the housekeeper, and he comes down here sometimes when MayBeth is working, but I don't think he rolls his own."

"When was the last time he was here? If this had been tossed here any earlier than last night, it would be wet by now or swept into the bay."

"I don't know for sure, but MayBeth usually comes on Fridays. Maybe Ben smokes."

"I'm hanging on to this." He slipped the cigarette into his pocket. "He knows you're staying at your mom's. He knows how to get here, and he tried to break in."

"And he knows you're here too—for now."

"You've been checking your texts? We know he has your number from Casey's phone."

She patted her jacket pocket. "All the time. He's gone quiet after weeks of harassing me."

"Then he was just trying to intimidate you into keeping quiet about your suspicions."

"Now he's afraid I'm going to find him out and report him. If he hadn't started murdering people, I wouldn't have had a clue to his identity."

"Those murders were always in his playbook—maybe not Tony's—but he wanted to cover his tracks and get rid of Wentworth and Casey. She could tie him to both Wentworth and the emails, and he wanted to erase that link. The only loose end left was you holding on to those emails for some reason he can't figure out."

"Believe me. I couldn't figure it out at first either, but now I know it was instinct that led me to hold on to them." She tucked her hand in his pocket. "And that instinct led you to me. It all happened for a reason."

He inserted his hand and folded it around hers. "I feel it, too. We're like puzzle pieces, and we both fill a part in this mosaic."

She pressed her arm against his as she hunched her shoulder. "I'm cold. Let's go inside, and I'll find someone to fix that window."

A phone buzzed and Cam dipped his hand into his other pocket. "That's yours."

Martha pulled out her phone and cupped a hand around the display to read the text. "It's my friend Farah. She's a translator who works with me."

"I'm assuming everyone at work knows what's going on with you."

"Yeah." She looked up from the phone. "Farah wants to meet for drinks tonight to tell me what's going on, what people are saying."

"Can she be trusted?"

"Farah? Absolutely."

"Then I think it's a good idea. Get the pulse of what's going on there."

"I think you're right." Martha cupped the phone with one hand and texted with her thumb.

She had two more exchanges with Farah and then pocketed the phone. "We're all set for eight o'clock tonight."

Cam took her hand. "Plenty of time to replace the glass in the window, get your locks changed and make a trip to and from my hotel."

"To and from?"

"To pick up my stuff and bring it here." He

pressed a kiss against her temple. "After what happened here this morning, you don't think I'm going to allow you to stay on your own, do you?"

Cam pulled her close on their walk back to the house, inhaling the crisp scent of the bay that clung to her hair. He didn't know how he was ever going to leave Martha on her own as long as this killer had her in his sights.

SECURITY BUSINESS AND errands ate up the rest of the afternoon. Martha had a locksmith change the locks to her town house, got the glass replaced in the sliding glass door and Cam moved from his hotel to Mom's house.

Too tired to cook and too frazzled to go out, they picked up a pizza on the way back to Mom's. Martha patted her full tummy and curled one leg beneath her on the sofa. "I was relieved to see that our friend hadn't made a return visit to my town house."

"Not that we know of, anyway. You should've followed your mother's example and wired that place with a security system."

"He probably would've disabled that like he did the one at the bar." She nudged the pizza box with the toe of her shoe. "There are two pieces left. Do you want them, or should I wrap them up and put them in the fridge?"

"People actually wrap and refrigerate leftover pizza instead of just eating it in the morning?"

"Ugh." She wrinkled her nose as she eyed the gooey cheese congealing on top of the slices.

Reaching forward and ripping the pieces apart, Cam said, "I'd better do them justice now."

As a shot of the Insider flashed on the muted TV screen, Martha lunged for the remote and turned up the volume. "I wonder if they have any suspects yet."

"You and I both know the police will never find the real killer."

They listened to the story for a minute, and then Martha muted the sound again. "They're still putting out the burglary story. Maybe they don't want to reveal the message on the table to the general public."

"Well, he did clean out the cash drawer and the safe to make it look good."

"And destroyed the security system."

"Good thing he did that or we'd be on it, front and center." Cam dragged a napkin across his mouth. "I haven't heard anything yet about Tony's extracurricular activities."

"Or his connection to Casey."

"Just another vicious murder in DC."

"Georgetown, and that's why it's getting so much air play."

"Is this bar we're going to tonight near the Insider?"

"Not far." Martha sniffed the air. "What is that smell? Tobacco? I've been smelling it on and off all day."

Cam reached across her and plucked his jacket from the arm of the sofa. "It's that cigarette I picked up by the boat dock. The tobacco is kind of sweet, isn't it?"

"And strong." She pushed up from the sofa. "I'll get you a plastic bag from the kitchen."

As she made a grab for the pizza box, Cam snatched up the last piece of pizza. "I'm saving this piece from the fate of being wrapped and stored."

She snorted. "A great sacrifice for you, I'm sure."

An hour later, they were on their way to another bar in Georgetown, and Martha hoped for a better outcome than last night.

She yawned as she pulled into a public parking lot on the crowded street. "I'm not sure I should have a drink tonight. I'm ready to fall asleep as it is."

"I wouldn't make any promises you can't keep." Cam tapped on the window to point out an empty parking space. "You may need a drink after listening to what your friend has to say."

They walked the two blocks to the waterfront bar hand in hand, and Martha could almost imagine they were on a regular date. She couldn't help noticing the admiring glances women threw at Cam, and she was just superficial enough that the attention to her date brought a smile to her face.

She tugged on Cam's hand as the bar came into view. "This is a date, right? You're not in Delta Force, you didn't track me down to interrogate me about the Denver emails, you never met Casey or saw Wentworth at my place."

"Just like we discussed." He opened the door for her and put his hand on her back as he whispered in her ear, "Do you see Farah?"

Martha swept the bar with her gaze and spotted Farah at a table with the guy she'd met on a dating website a few months ago—the married guy. "She's over there, and..."

Cam didn't give her a chance to finish her sentence. He crooked an arm around her neck and pulled her around for a kiss on the mouth.

For a few seconds Martha forgot she was standing in a crowded bar, forgot she had a three-time killer stalking her, forgot she was going to lose Cam in a week.

Her arm curled around his waist, and she

sagged against him as a pool of heat ached between her legs.

He ended the long kiss, punctuated by another peck on the lips. “There. That should put any doubt about this being date night to rest.”

Martha blinked and adjusted her glasses. She cleared her throat. “Right.”

She yanked on his sleeve. “What I was going to say before you ambushed me is that Farah is here with her scumbag boyfriend.”

“He’s a scumbag?”

“He’s married.”

“Oh, that kind of scumbag.” He rubbed her back. “You weren’t planning to get top secret with Farah anyway, were you?”

“No.”

“Then let’s see if she can tell you what they’re saying about you in the office.” He nudged her back, and she led him to Farah’s table.

Farah rose from her chair, her wide, dark eyes darting from Martha to Cam. She gave Martha a one-armed hug and said, “You take a day off work and collect a boyfriend along the way?”

Martha kissed her friend’s cheek. “Farah, this is Cam. Cam, this is Farah and Scott.”

Everyone shook hands, and Martha and Cam

crowded around the small table, as Cam craned his neck. "Waiters coming by?"

"Not often enough." Scott raised his almost empty bottle of beer. "I need to hit the men's room. I'll swing by the bar on the way and get us a round. Farah?"

She covered her wineglass with her hand. "I'm good."

Cam tapped Scott's bottle. "I'll have one of these."

Martha pointed to Farah's glass of wine. "And I'll make it easy and have a glass of white wine, thanks."

Scott kissed Farah on the top of the head. "Be right back."

"Thanks, babe." Wiggling her fingers over her shoulder, Farah flicked back her hair. "I'm glad you came out, Martha. I just wanted to give you a heads-up about work. First of all, are you okay? My God, to find Wentworth dead in your town house and then Casey the next day. I can't even imagine what you're going through."

And Farah didn't even know about Tony. Martha shot a look beneath her lashes at Cam. "It's been a pretty rough few days. What are they saying at the office? What's *Gage* saying?"

"Just, you know." Farah swirled her wine in

the glass. "Lots of gossip about the congressman and your roommate."

Martha narrowed her eyes. "What's the real reason Proffit asked me to take a few days off?"

"I don't know." Farah hunched forward and twisted her head toward Cam. "Is he okay?"

"You can say anything in front of Cam."

Farah's tongue darted out of her mouth in a quick sweep of her lips. "Martha, they're looking at your computer."

Martha's jaw dropped, and a tickle of fear crept up her neck. "D-did they remove it from my cubicle."

Cam pressed his knee against hers and she welcomed the contact, although it did nothing to alleviate the panic galloping through her veins.

"No, but they've been in your cubicle a few times—all hush-hush. What else would they be doing in there?"

Cam asked, "Who's they? Who's been in Martha's cube?"

"Gage, Proffit and that tech guy." Farah tapped a fingernail against her glass. "Sebastian Forsythe, the one you dated a few times."

"That's not good." Martha grabbed Farah's glass and took a gulp of wine.

"You don't have anything to hide, do you,

Martha? No, of course you don't, but if the Agency is looking at your work computer that may not matter."

"You're right. It may not matter. Thanks for clueing me in, Farah."

She nodded and then put a finger to her lips as she glanced to the side. "Zip it."

Martha looked up to see Scott with three drinks gathered in his hands.

"Success." He placed the drinks on the table in a huddle, and then slid them to their owners. "Wine, beer, beer. I can go for another round if you need me to."

Farah squeezed his hand. "Thanks, babe. Maybe later. Let's toast."

"To Mondays." Scott leaned in and clinked his bottle to Martha's glass, and she instinctively drew away.

She'd never liked Farah's taste in men. She'd met Scott just a few times, but any guy who claimed to have an arrangement with his wife raised a red flag with her. She gave Scott a weak smile and took a sip of her wine. Cam had been right. She might need the whole glass to get through this get-together.

"Oh my God, did you hear about that bartender who was murdered during a robbery? It happened not far from here." Farah twisted the gold chain around her neck with her fingers. "Terrible."

"I did see that on the news." Martha shook her head. "Why'd the guy have to kill the bartender?"

"Maybe he didn't expect the bartender to be there, and he didn't want the bartender to ID him." Scott ran a thumbnail through the damp label on his bottle.

"Well, it was probably all for nothing anyway. I know that area, and there are CCTVs in all the bars." Farah pointed to a corner of the ceiling. "Probably in here, too."

"The robber took care of the cameras." Martha picked up her glass for another sip of wine, and someone kicked her under the table.

She choked on her wine and ended up taking a deeper gulp. She avoided looking at Cam. Who else would kick her?

"Took care of the cameras?" Farah tilted her head to one side.

Scott asked, "You mean disabled them? We didn't hear that."

Martha could've kicked herself—in the same spot Cam had kicked her. She'd better stick to translating because she clearly didn't have the makings of a spy.

"I think we heard something like that on the news before we left." Cam dragged his napkin over a few drops of wine on the table in front of Martha. “Do you follow football, Scott?”

The men talked football while Farah filled Martha in on other office gossip.

Several minutes later, Scott patted his front shirt pocket. “I’m going to head out to the deck for a smoke. Join me, Cam?”

“I don’t smoke, but I do need to hit the men’s room.” Cam scooted back from the table and winked. “We’ll leave you ladies to exchange secrets if you want.”

Cam and Scott walked several feet together until Scott peeled off for the deck on the side of the bar, and Cam continued to the back and the restrooms.

Farah bent her head to Martha’s and whispered, “Is it those emails, Martha? I didn’t want to say anything in front of Cam, but do you think Proffit knows you copied those emails onto a flash drive?”

“I don’t know how he could…unless someone told him.”

“Not me, I swear.” Farah drew a cross over her heart with one long fingernail. “Did you tell someone else?”

“No, but…” She snapped her mouth shut as she saw Scott coming in from the patio. “That was fast.”

“Oh, he’s trying to quit, so he doesn’t smoke

his cig all the way down. Screwy method if you ask me." Farah rolled her eyes and touched her glass to Martha's.

Martha cupped her wineglass with one hand and swirled another sip of the oaky chardonnay in her mouth, her eyebrows knitting over her nose as she followed Scott's progress back to their table.

Even as Cam appeared several feet behind Scott with a bottle of beer in each hand, Martha pinned her gaze to Scott, tracking his every movement. He stuffed something, a pouch, in the pocket of his jacket.

Martha jerked her head once and allowed the wine to run down the back of her throat. That pouch could be anything. Maybe it wasn't even a pouch. It didn't have to be loose tobacco, and plenty of people didn't smoke their cigarettes all the way down to the butt. He probably wanted to get back to Farah.

Eyeing her half-empty wineglass, Martha pushed it away from her as Scott reached their table.

He leaned in to kiss Farah on the mouth, and she shooed him away with both hands. "You know I can't stand smoking. I grew up with just about every member of my family lighting up, and I can't stand it—especially that tobacco and especially those roll-your-own cancer sticks."

Martha froze. This time when Scott sat down and pulled his chair up to the table, instead of moving away from him, she moved closer and inhaled deeply.

Her heart slammed against her rib cage. The odor of the tobacco from his breath caused a cold dread to snake up her spine.

Chapter Twelve

Cam placed the beers on the table and nodded to Scott. He didn't want to stay much longer, but he owed Scott a round. Unless Farah had dropped a bombshell in the past ten minutes, she'd told Martha everything she knew about the office. Wasn't much Martha could do about it now.

Someone kicked his shin under the table, and he shifted his leg to the side. Then Martha scooted her chair toward him and dug her fingernails into his thigh—at least he hoped those were Martha's fingers so close to his crotch.

Picking up his beer, he met her gaze above the bottle and almost choked on the liquid running down his throat. Her pale face and her lips pressed together in a thin line made his stomach drop. Had Farah delivered more bad news?

Martha made a grab for her wineglass and knocked it over. She jerked back from the table. "Sorry."

Scott tossed his napkin on top of the spreading pool of wine. "Do you want another?"

"No!" Martha shoved her chair back from the table. "No, thank you. I think we'd better be going. I—I have to let my mom's dog out."

"Your mom has a dog?"

As Farah tilted her head, Cam drew his eyebrows together. What had lit a fire under Martha? Farah didn't seem to know.

Martha jumped up from the table. "Thanks so much for the heads-up, Farah. If anything else happens, let me know. Hopefully, I'll be back at work next week once the Agency realizes I wasn't at all involved in Casey and the Congressman's relationship."

"Sounds like a movie of the week, Casey and the Congressman." Farah stood up and gave Martha a one-armed hug and shook Cam's hand. "Nice to meet you."

Scott stood up, as well, and everyone said their goodbyes, which couldn't happen fast enough for Cam. Something had obviously happened to spook Martha when he'd been absent, but that something hadn't come from Farah.

Cam slid Martha's coat and purse from the back of her chair. "We'll have to do this again."

As he handed Martha's purse to her, she elbowed him in the ribs, and he sucked in a breath. He helped her into her coat and she grabbed his arm, practically dragging him out of the bar.

When they hit the sidewalk, Martha folded her arms and continued her quick pace.

He bumped her shoulder. "What's going on? Where are we going? Your mother doesn't even have a dog."

She didn't say one word until they got into the car and closed the doors. Then she turned to him and grabbed his sleeve.

"Farah's boyfriend? Scott?"

He nodded. "Yeah?"

"He's our guy."

"Our guy? The one who hacked you?"

"The one who killed three people."

"How do you know that?" His gaze darted to the side mirror.

"Did you smell him when he came back to the table?"

"I don't usually make a habit out of sniffing other dudes."

She slugged his shoulder. "I'm serious, Cam. He smelled sweetish, just like that cigarette you picked up on the boat dock."

"Same tobacco?"

She licked her lips. "It's more than that. He rolls his own cigarettes, and when he came back from his smoke after just a few minutes,

Farah told me he's trying to quit and smokes only half his cigarette."

"The one on the dock was only half smoked." He rubbed his knuckles against his jaw. "Maybe you're onto something."

She closed her eyes and pressed her fingers against her temples. "I think I am. It's too coincidental."

"When did Farah start dating him?"

"About four months ago. Met him online, and he told her he was married right away. She's not looking for something permanent, so that didn't bother her."

"He told her he was married to explain why he didn't bring her to his place or introduce her to his friends."

Martha started the car but didn't make a move. "He started dating her to get close to me. Just like he ordered Casey to keep an eye on me. Everyone around me is proving to be false."

He grabbed her hand. "Not me. Do you think Farah's in on it? She could've been the one who identified you to be the conduit of those emails."

"No way. Farah wouldn't do that."

"That's what you thought about Casey, too." He entwined his fingers with hers. "It's like they're forming a snare around you, Martha. They wanted people on the inside, watching you—from work and from home."

"That doesn't make sense." The chattering of her teeth swallowed up her last word.

"Sure it does." He turned up the heat in the car. "On some level you know it. You recognized the smell of that cigarette when it had been in my pocket. It struck a chord with you because you'd smelled it before—on him."

"If it's all true, if Scott's the killer, we can't leave Farah to him. I'm not going to allow her to be alone with a killer."

He reached over and cut the engine, and then grabbed the door handle. "I wish you would've told me this sooner, right outside the bar. I could've confronted him then."

"What are you doing?"

He cranked his head over his shoulder. "I'm going back. He's right under our noses. I'm not going to let him slip through my grasp now after trying to ID him for days."

"Wait." She put her hand on his back. "Do we really want him to know we're onto him? What do you think he was planning in there? He *did* get us our drinks."

Cam ran his tongue around the inside of his mouth. "What would be the point in drugging us in a public place, in front of his supposed girlfriend?"

"Maybe he wanted to drug us for later. Knock

us out at my mom's house and break in without disturbing us."

"That's some long-acting drug."

"I don't know." She flattened her palm against her chest. "You do know that he arranged this meeting tonight, don't you? Somehow, someway, he got Farah to invite me out."

"I agree. None of this is coincidence." He pushed open the door. "And I'm going to find out why. I'm going to find out who put him up to this, and why they want to bring down Major Denver."

"Cam!"

The urgency burned in his gut. On some logical level he knew Martha was right. Why show their hand now? But he might never get a crack at this guy again. He was two blocks away. He had to make a move.

Cam broke into a jog, even as he heard Martha calling behind him. He dodged a couple of cars to cross the street to the restaurant and burst through the doors.

The chairs where the four of them had sat were empty, the table still littered with their glasses and bottles. He threaded his way through the bar and loomed over the table.

"Forget something?"

He spun around and almost knocked into the waitress. "The other couple, they left?"

"Right after you did." She balanced her tray on her hip and repeated her question. "Forget something?"

"It's all right. I'll call them later." Cam backed up to the table and wrapped his fingers around the neck of Scott's beer bottle. He shuffled around the waitress, keeping the bottle behind him. "Thanks."

Outside the bar when he reached the street corner, Martha pounced on him. "What were you doing? How could confronting him in public possibly work?"

"Don't worry. They'd left." He presented the beer bottle with a flourish and held it in front of Martha's face. "And I snagged this."

"His fingerprints."

"Exactly. I have a buddy with the PD in Virginia who can help out with the prints."

She slipped her fingers in the back pocket of his jeans as they walked to the car. "Scott's playing with fire. How did he know we wouldn't be able to ID him?"

"He probably felt secure since he was obviously wearing a disguise when he met with Casey and Tony, and he had a mask on this morning at your mom's house. When Tony described him with the beard and glasses, we already figured he'd donned a disguise."

"We can't prove anything based on a tobacco brand, Cam."

"Who knows? We could even be wrong about him, but I doubt it."

When they reached the car, Martha leaned against it, shoving her hands in her pockets. "Farah. We can't leave her alone with him."

"Would they go back to her place?"

"They never go to his place. He's conveniently married, remember?"

"We can't go charging into Farah's place. We need a plan." Cam rubbed his hands together against the chill of the night. "But let's do it in the car with the engine running and the heat blasting."

Once in the car, Cam turned to Martha. "Do you know where Farah lives?"

"A town house not far from here."

"We could drop by on some pretext—you left your phone at the bar, or something work related. If Scott's still there, you could get Farah alone. Maybe you could warn her against him."

She worried her bottom lip. "If he's at her place and you see him again, will you be able to control yourself? You charged back to the bar, ready to get some answers from him."

"If he is there, it might be the perfect opportunity to get some answers." Cam drummed his thumbs against the dashboard. "He'd be in a private place. I could let him know we have his prints and are going to the police with our suspicions."

"Like you said before, we have nothing to tie him to the three murders. Heck, the cops aren't even calling Congressman Wentworth's death a murder." She rolled her eyes. "I don't think a cigarette is going to do the trick, do you? We never even reported his attempted break-in to the police."

"We know that, but he doesn't. It might give us a little leverage with him. He's gonna realize he dropped a cigarette at your place, so that'll ring true." He slapped his hand against the dashboard. "It's worth a try. I'm not letting this guy slip away."

Martha threw the car into gear. "I agree, but I don't want anyone getting hurt."

"Nobody's going to get hurt." He ran a hand down her thigh. "Especially not you."

"Or Farah."

"Or Farah."

"Or you."

"Got it."

Ten minutes later, Martha parallel parked at the curb and pointed to a row of town houses. "Farah's is on the end."

Cam twisted around and peered out the back window. "Quiet street."

"Well, it is all residential and it's a weeknight." She turned off the engine and blew out a breath. "Ready?"

"We're ready." He patted his jacket pocket, feeling the hard outline of his weapon.

Martha's gaze followed the gesture. "Nobody's getting hurt, right?"

"Would you really care if Scott-Ben-Patriot got hurt? He murdered three people—that we know of—and he's after you and using Farah, putting her in danger."

"I know you're right, but you can't just run around shooting people based on a half-smoked cigarette—even if you are a hotshot D-Boy." She touched his face. "I'm more worried about you than him. I don't want you getting into any trouble."

He captured her fingers and kissed the tips. "And I don't want you getting into any trouble. Nobody's going to know you took those emails."

"My hand may be forced in the end if we want to put a stop to this guy." Closing her eyes, she sighed.

"You're not going to end up like your father." He squeezed her fingers before releasing them. "Let's go."

When Cam slammed the passenger door, a dog popped up at a window of a town house and barked. “At least someone’s on guard around here.”

“Let me do the talking.” Martha pocketed her keys and took the lead to Farah’s place on the corner.

This neighborhood lacked the understated elegance of Martha’s with the fronts of the town houses closer to the edge of the sidewalk, but still nobody glanced out their windows at them as they passed by.

The area didn’t scream high crime, but Cam shoved his hand in his jacket pocket and caressed the handle of his gun anyway. The silence of the street had him coiling his muscles in expectation of…something.

Martha drew up to the steps of Farah’s town house and pulled back her shoulders. “This is it.”

Cam looked over Martha’s head at the glow from the front window, the drapes tugged close, keeping the warmth and light from spilling onto the sidewalk. No light gleamed from the window to the left of this one, and the town house seemed draped in silence like the rest of the block.

Martha breezed up the steps and rang the

doorbell. Shifting to the side, she said, "I want her to see me from the peephole."

Cam kept his eye in the square of light that was the front window, searching for movement or shadows.

He swallowed. "I don't think she's home, Martha."

"Not home?" Martha jabbed at the doorbell again. "Where would they be?"

Cam lifted a stiff shoulder. "Don't know."

Martha stepped back, tilting her head to scan the windows of the second story. "No lights on up there. Maybe they're in bed."

"Farah and Scott?"

Martha stuck her finger in her open mouth to mimic gagging. "I know. It makes me sick to think about it."

"Maybe you should call her." Cam's jaw ached with the insidious tension that had crawled through him ever since he stepped from the car. "Call her."

Martha shot him a sharp glance and then fumbled with her phone. She tapped the screen and listened for several seconds. "It's Martha. I'm on your front porch. Something I need to ask you, so give me a call when you get this or let me in if you're home."

"This place has a side door and a back door?"

"Back door, I think." Martha folded her arms, clutching her purse to her side. "Why?"

"I want you to go back to the car, Martha. Just sit inside and wait for me. I'm going to do a quick check."

Her eyes got round behind her glasses. "Why?"

"Just want to make sure."

"Make sure about what, that Farah's not dead behind those doors? Like Casey? Like Tony?"

Her voice had risen to a squeal, and Cam put a finger to her soft lips. "We came here to check on Farah, didn't we? To make sure she was okay. I'm gonna do that now, and you're gonna go back to the car and wait for me."

He put his hands around her waist and twirled her toward the car as if they were on the dance floor. "It's just a precaution. I'm sure she's fine."

She cranked her head over her shoulder and covered her mouth. "What if we endangered Farah's life by taking off like that? Maybe Scott realized we'd made the connection. I said my mom had a dog. If Scott was the one prowling around this morning, he's going to know there's no dog at that house."

He stroked her back. "That's not a given.

Could be a lapdog, one of those little fur balls. Don't think that way. I won't be long."

He watched as she stumbled toward the car, and then he slipped around the side of the town house. If something had happened to Farah, Martha didn't need to bear witness to it.

He crept up to the first window and touched the glass with his nose, squinting to see through the gap in the curtains. He saw a slice of neat, undisturbed kitchen, and the threshold of the living room beyond.

He tried raising the window, but it didn't budge. If he did break in and discovered Farah and Scott in bed, he'd have a lot of explaining to do—especially if Scott really was just some cheatin' dog and not a killer.

Hunching forward, he made his way to the back of the town house where a short gate blocked his path. As he reached over the top to feel for the latch, he froze.

The eerie silence of the neighborhood had been broken by something much worse—Martha's scream.

Chapter Thirteen

About five feet from the car, Martha aimed the remote to unlock the doors. A sick feeling had been gnawing at her gut ever since Cam's true purpose for searching Farah's place and sending her to the car had dawned on her.

If anything happened to Farah, she'd never forgive herself. How many people had to pay the price for her stupidity of snagging those emails for herself?

A pair of headlights flooded the street, and Martha caught her breath. Maybe Scott and Farah had come back and if so, she'd have to waylay them out here until Cam finished his search—and then somehow explain where Cam had gone and why.

The car slowed down, and Martha ran her tongue along her bottom lip as she recognized Farah's vehicle. She whispered, "C'mon, Cam."

The car double-parked next to her own, and

just as Martha pasted a fake smile on her face, the driver's door sprang open.

"Hey, Farah, we—"

Martha broke off as the figure moved toward her, the black ski mask covering his face. She tripped backward, throwing her arms out to her sides to recover her balance.

The man circled behind her and took advantage of her unsteadiness. One strong arm curled around her chest, dragging her to the street and the idling car—Farah's car.

She used her last burst of air to scream. She dug her heels into the pavement. They scraped against it as her attacker pulled her to the street. When he reached Farah's car, he pulled open the passenger door and scrambled in backward, pulling her along with him even as she clawed at his arm and kicked at his legs.

"Hey, hey!"

Martha sobbed as Cam's shouts echoed in the night.

The man holding her grunted as he landed behind the wheel, and he threw the car into gear. As the car jerked into motion, he growled, "Stay out of this, or I'll be forced to kill you."

He'd released his hold on her, but the car was now in motion and her body was half in and half out, one foot inches off the ground.

She felt rather than saw Cam launch himself

at the moving car. With one hand, he grasped onto the door as it swung wide, his other hand clutching his weapon pointed futilely at the ground. His legs scrambled beneath him, as they tried to keep pace with the moving vehicle.

Martha screamed again as the car veered toward a pole. The masked man would crush Cam if he could.

Through his panting, Cam said, "Get out, Martha. You have to get out. Fall on me."

The driver punched the gas pedal, and the car leaped forward. The car door swung back again.

Martha braced her foot against the seat as her attacker made a grab for her leg. She twisted and kicked him in the side.

Her new position gave her a view of the back seat, and she choked. "Cam, Cam."

"Out now!"

Cam yanked her by the arm, and she felt suspended in air for a second before landing on top of Cam's solid body. His arms wrapped around her, and they rolled together for several feet along a stretch of foliage.

They came to rest against a rise that broke their momentum, and Martha squeezed a painful breath from her lungs.

"Are you all right?" Cam's hands brushed across her face.

"I—I think so." She heaved a strangled sob.

"My God. He was trying to get you into the car." He smoothed the hair back from her face. "I should've never left you."

"Cam." She bunched fistfuls of his jacket in her hands. "He had Farah."

"What do you mean? That was her car?"

"He had her in the back seat. She was knocked out or..." She buried her face against his chest.

Cam struggled to sit up, brushing bits of leaves and twigs from his sleeves. "We have to call the police now. We'll stick as close to the truth as possible, but we need to report Farah's kidnapping and his attempted kidnapping of you."

"He warned me again. When it became clear he wasn't going to succeed in his abduction, he told me to back off. He said something weird."

Cam curled his arm beneath her back, and she winced as she sat up. When a car drove by, they both hunched toward the ground, but the driver rolled by without even noticing them.

"What was weird?"

"He told me to stay out of this or he'd be forced to kill me." Martha combed her fingers through her tangled hair. "Forced to kill me. He doesn't want to, but why? If he took me out now, he wouldn't have to worry about my finding anything else that Casey left behind for me."

"How would that look?" Cam rose to his knees, and cupped her elbow to help her up along with him. "A CIA translator is the conduit for a batch of emails implicating a Delta Force commander in colluding with the enemy. That translator's roommate kills herself after her congressman lover dies, and then the translator accidentally dies? Disappears? Is murdered? If Wentworth's death wasn't on the FBI's radar, your death and Casey's would definitely put it there."

"This is all blowing up for him and his plans to make the emails seem like some concerned patriot looking out for the good of the country."

"You're blowing it up for him. You and your out of left field decision to keep those emails." Cam touched her nose. "What happened to your glasses?"

"I don't know. I can't even remember if I had them when he pulled me into Farah's car." She bunched a fist against her midsection. "What are we going to do about Farah? He can't kill her, either. Even though she didn't receive the emails, she's a CIA translator."

"With no connection to Casey or Wentworth

or as you just mentioned, the emails. He could make her death look like an accident."

"But we're friends." Martha clung to Cam as if she were clinging to hope about Farah's safety. "That would look suspicious."

"If he doesn't kill her, she's going to report him."

"Maybe not." Martha took a wobbling step and grabbed Cam's arm for support. "If he drugged her wine and took her to the car where she passed out, she's not going to know any of this happened."

"Unless we call the police right now and tell them what we witnessed."

"Maybe that's not the way to go right now. We'd force his hand if he we do that."

"We have to go to the authorities at some point with what we know, Martha, or what would've been the whole point in all this? We have to let them know the emails were a plant to discredit Major Denver."

She slipped her hand in his pocket as they limped back to her car parked down the block from Farah's place. "What happened to your gun?"

"Dropped it." He pointed to the ground. "That's why I'm walking with my head down."

"What a pair we are." She leaned her head

against his shoulder. “I guess Scott knew I realized his identity in the bar.”

“Yeah, well, don’t beat yourself up over that. If I’d put two and two together about those cigarettes, I probably would’ve assaulted him right then and there, and that wouldn’t have been smart.”

“It probably would’ve saved Farah.”

Cam stopped suddenly and she bumped into him.

“Found it.” He stooped to pick up his weapon, which had landed in the gutter of the street.

“You haven’t seen a pair of glasses down there, have you?”

“I’ve been looking.”

They reached the car, and Martha shivered when she saw the black skid marks in the street. If Cam hadn’t come to her rescue, she’d be God knew where right now with a killer and a comatose Farah in the back seat of her car.

Cam swooped down and snatched up the keys she’d dropped during the attack. He dangled them from his fingers. “Are you okay to drive?”

She tapped her temple. “No glasses. You take the wheel.” She looked up and down the empty street. “I can’t believe all that commotion didn't prompt someone to call the police. Didn't anyone hear me scream?"

"I did." He opened the passenger door and helped her in. "That's all that matters."

As Cam walked around to the driver's side, two more cars drove by and Martha slid down in her seat.

He slammed the door and gripped the top of the steering wheel, stretching his arms in front of him. "We need to make a decision about Farah. She's incapacitated in the clutches of a killer."

"On the other hand..." She put one hand over her mouth. "Did I really say that after what you stated as the obvious?"

"This is me you're talking to, Martha." He thumped his chest with his fist. "I understand the gray areas. Let me finish your thought. On the other hand, if Farah's in the dark about being drugged, or kidnapped or Scott's wild ride with us clinging to an open car door, she's still safe and maybe we don't have to do anything at all right now to help her."

Martha nodded, happy that Cam had understood her coldhearted statement. "That's what I mean. Scott could take her to a hotel and tell her she passed out, got sick, whatever. He wouldn't have to harm her at that point because she never would even know she'd been in danger—except for us and if we call the police..."

Cam squeezed the bridge of his nose. "That's our dilemma."

"Cam." Martha spread her hands in front of her and inspected an abrasion on her knuckle. "I think it might be time for me to call an attorney. Gage at work was joking, but I *should* call my father's attorney. He's a family friend."

"Are you thinking of coming clean about the emails?" He traced a scratch on the back of her hand to her wrist.

"I think it's the only way now to protect Farah and tell the police and the FBI everything about Wentworth, Casey and Tony. I haven't heard any news about an autopsy for Wentworth, but they're still calling it a heart attack and Casey's still a suicide. The police haven't asked me anything else about her death or friends or state of mind."

"I don't want you to get in trouble, Martha."

"I did that all by myself." Her nose tingled, and she swiped the back of her hand across it.

"You tried to go through the right channels about your suspicions, but it didn't work. Nobody would listen to you."

"Coming clean would also help your cause. This guy, these people, have gone to great lengths, even murder, to set this all up and then deal with the loose ends. It will prompt an investigation of the emails and Major Denver."

"Like you said before. It still won't clear his name."

"But the doubt will be out there. What other evidence was fabricated against him? The CIA will have to take a second look." She dragged her purse from the floor of the back seat and fished her phone from the side pocket. Scanning through her contacts, she said, "I'm not sure I have Sam Prescott's number on my phone, but it will be on my mom's computer."

"Whoa. You're going too fast." Cam splayed his hands across the steering wheel. "Don't you think you should talk to someone first? Get some advice?"

"That's why I'm going to call Sam." She pointed the corner of her phone at Cam.

"I suppose there's no point in waiting for Scott to bring Farah back home." Cam pulled away from the curb and made a U-turn in the middle of the street.

Martha's phone buzzed in her hand and she jerked it in front of her face. "I-it's Farah. It must be him."

"Answer it and put it on speaker."

"Farah?" Martha pressed a hand against her chest and her thundering heart.

"What's up? What's so urgent?" Hearing

Farah's voice, clear if slow, sent a rush of relief flowing through Martha's body.

"You're okay?"

Cam put a hand on her arm and shook his head.

He was right. If Farah didn't know she was in danger, that just might save her. Her captor wouldn't have to kill her.

"Kinda woozy, but yeah. What's wrong? I got your voice mail from earlier. What was so urgent that you had to come out to my place?"

Martha cleared her throat. "Cam thought he left his cell phone at the bar and figured you and… Scott might've picked it up."

"I didn't notice any phone. We left pretty soon after you did. Are you going to tell me about Cam? He's a hot hunk of man, girl."

Martha snuck a peak at Cam, who rolled his eyes. He'd probably heard that line a million times.

"Where are you, Farah?" Cam poked her in her sore ribs. "A-Are you home now?"

"No. Scott treated me to a hotel suite. I was so out of it, he thought a nice spa day tomorrow would make me feel better. Isn't that sweet?"

Martha gritted her teeth. "He's still married, Farah. You need to get out of that relationship."

Farah giggled. "Shh. You're on speakerphone and Scott just heard that. That's just Martha, baby. You know this suits me just fine."

A chill snaked up Martha's back. She knew whose idea it was for Farah to broadcast this call.

Scott shouted from the background. "You're totally right, Martha. Maybe Farah and I should end this relationship—for good, but we'll enjoy ourselves for now. I'm not going to hurt Farah, and she's free to leave me whenever she wants—after I pamper her for a few days."

"Aww, see what you did, Martha? You let me worry about my own affairs…and you can concentrate on that handful of man you have. By the way, did Cam ever find his phone?"

"He did, thanks."

"Okay, then. I'll see you later."

"Be…have fun."

"We will." Farah ended the call on another giggle.

Martha cupped the dead phone in her hands. "That call was a message to us. Farah is safe… for now, as long as she doesn't discover his true motives."

"He can't keep her at that hotel forever."

"Two days. I think she's taking a few days off this week for Thanksgiving, and as long as he has her there, we can't call the police." She tucked her hands between her bouncing knees. "He as good as threatened her."

"Do you still want to consult that attorney?"

"I have to." Her voice shook, and she shot a sideways glance at Cam to see if he noticed.

He reached over and pinched her chin. "I'm sorry you lost your glasses."

"I have contacts at my mom's."

By the time they reached her mother's house, it was past midnight. Martha's knees trembled as Cam opened the front door for her, and it wasn't due to the aches and pains racking her body from the tumble out of the car.

Would she and Cam share a bed again tonight? Would they make love? The clicking clock on their time together echoed in her head, marked her every breath.

Once she contacted Sam and came clean, she might lose her job, she might go to jail, but none of that mattered as much as the looming threat of losing Cam.

Could a member of Delta Force ever be involved with a spy, a federal criminal?

Cam tapped the alarm system. "Arm it, even though our guy will be spending the night somewhere else."

"Unless he drugs Farah again and sneaks out." She punched in the code for the alarm system and tossed her purse into a chair. "How long does he expect to buy my silence by holding a threat over Farah's head? Once I go to the authorities and tell all, Farah will know everything."

Cam walked to the kitchen with a hitch in his step and reached for a glass.

"I didn't even ask if you were okay." She followed him into the kitchen and wrapped her arms around his waist from behind. "You took the brunt of that tumble from the car."

He lifted his broad shoulders. "I took it like a football tackle. I know how to fall and roll."

"With a gangly woman attached to your body?"

He threw back the water and kissed her mouth with wet lips. "That was the best part. Should we undress each other slowly and inspect our bodies for injuries?"

"Is that a new line?"

"I don't know. Will it work?"

"You don't need any lines to get me into bed, Cam Sutton." She skimmed her hands across his face and flicked his earlobe, which sported a spot of dried blood. "But I do think we need a soak in the bathtub first to clean all our boo-boos."

"Is *that* a new line, 'cause I gotta tell you, discussing my…boo-boos is a total turnoff."

She rested her head against his chest. Her lips formed a smile, but a tear leaked from the corner of her eye and she sniffled.

Drawing away, he wedged a knuckle beneath her chin and tilted back her head. “I’m sorry. Boos-boos are a turn on. Gives me a chance to take care of you.”

She sniffed, but he coaxed a bigger smile from her. “When I’m in federal prison sharing a cell block with my dad, will the army forbid you from fraternizing with an enemy of the state?”

He snorted. “I just might be in the next cell block over.”

“What do you mean?” She wrinkled her nose. “You haven’t done anything wrong?”

He lifted one eyebrow. “Really? I have knowledge about your theft of those emails and failed to disclose that intelligence. I helped you clean evidence off your computer. I stumbled upon a murder scene and didn’t report it. I could go on, but I’m sure your attorney can fill you in.”

Her chest tightened as she dug her fingernails into Cam’s biceps. “I can’t do it. I can’t do that to you.”

He scooped his hands through her hair. “You do what you have to do to stay safe, Martha.”

“Not if it’s going to put you in jeopardy.”

He pulled her head down and kissed the top. "Let's talk to that lawyer first…but not before we take a bath and check out each other's bodies."

She took the glass from his hand and drank the rest of the water. "Deal."

Just in case Cam thought she was kidding about the bath, she threw open the door of the master bathroom and cranked on the faucets for the sunken, oval tub while he prowled around downstairs, securing every door and window in the place.

By the time he joined her upstairs, Martha had a tub full of steaming, scented bubbles and candles.

He hung on the doorjamb and whistled. "I should've brought up two glasses of wine."

"That would probably put me to sleep, and I'm still trying to get the taste of that other wine out of my mouth."

Two steps took him into the room, and he slid his hands beneath her robe and squeezed her shoulders. "Do you still think he put something in your wine?"

"He sure put something in Farah's."

"But you feel okay? No strange aftereffects?"

"I'll feel better once I crawl into that warm water." She dropped her phone on top of a basket full of rolled-up towels and dipped her toe past the bubbles and into the water. "It's perfect."

He slipped the robe from her shoulders and kissed the side of her neck. "You're perfect."

Cam shrugged off his clothes, they shared a long kiss before sliding into the tub together. Despite Cam's size, the cavernous bathtub allowed him to stretch out. He settled her between his legs and ran his hands gingerly across her back.

"You're going to have a few bruises back here."

"I'm glad that's all. I expected some broken bones." She scooped up a handful of bubbles and scattered them with a breath from her pursed lips. "Do you think Farah's okay?"

"He doesn't want to harm her. He doesn't want to harm you."

"Cam, why do you think he's still here? He planted the emails with me, or an associate did, he took care of his loose ends by killing Wentworth, Casey and Tony. What more does he want? He knows, or at least he thinks he knows, that I'm not going anywhere with the info I have. Where would I go? Implicating him implicates me."

"He's still looking for whatever Casey left behind." Cam's hands made waves in the water pooling over her belly. "He knows you don't have it, and he wants to find it before you do."

"We searched through her stuff. There's nothing there that implicates him or anyone else. What could it be?"

"Maybe it was just his identity, and now that we have that—or at least who he's pretending to be—he has Farah. I guess he believes that will stop us from turning him in."

"Well, he's right, but how long can he keep her? Like you said before, he can't make her stay in that hotel forever. She'll have her spa day tomorrow, and another few days, but what then?"

His hands floated toward her breasts, and he cupped them. "You're safe. Farah's somewhat safe, and you're going to talk to your father's attorney tomorrow. There's nothing left for us to do tonight. Let me make you feel better."

She succumbed to the sweet kisses and gentle caresses that slowly stoked the embers of her passion, so different from the fiery explosions of last night.

By the time they returned to her bedroom, Cam had to pour her limp body onto the sheets. He whispered in her ear, "You're still going to need some ibuprofen tomorrow."

She burrowed under the covers. "Bring it on. I feel ready for anything right now."

The bed dipped as Cam snuggled in behind her. His arm draped heavily across her midsection, and his leg hitched over her hip. She felt engulfed by him, and she soaked up the feeling, trying to drown out the thought of his departure that echoed in her head like a hollow drumbeat.

The buzzing of her cell replaced the dirge, and her lids flew open. "It has to be him."

Cam bolted upright and made a grab for her phone. He squinted at the display. "It's not Farah. Unknown number."

"It's him." She snapped her fingers, and Cam held out the phone to her. She tapped in her password and swiped open the text.

"Is it Scott?"

Tilting her head to the side, Martha blew a wisp of hair from her eyes as she read the text. A cold fist squeezed her heart, and she dropped the phone with a gasp.

Cam snatched it up. "Is it him? Is it that bastard?"

"No. It's a text from a dead woman."

Chapter Fourteen

Martha's pale face stood out in the darkness of the room. Cam fumbled with the light switch on the wall to turn on the ceiling fans above the bed, and brought the phone close to his face.

"Casey? Is it from Casey?"

"H-how can that be?"

The letters on the display swam before Cam's eyes, the words they formed, nothing but gibberish to his brain. "What did she write? What does it say?'

"Read it." Martha had folded her hands together, her knuckles as white as the sheets beneath them, seemingly incapable or unwilling to take the phone from him.

He made another pass at the jumbled words on the screen, and then shoved the phone between her wrists. "I can't, damn it. I can't read it, Martha."

His words shocked her out of her stupor,

and she picked up the cell and read aloud the words from Casey. "'Martha, it's me, Casey. If you get this message after I've disappeared, I locked myself out. I'm sorry.'"

"Locked herself out?" Cam tipped his head back against the headboard and stared at the ceiling. "If she locked herself out, she'd get the key from the zippered cover of the lawn chair, but we already looked there. She must be referring to the message she left you about Tony."

"Did she even send that message, Cam? How? How do we know it came from her?"

"She scheduled the text to be delivered at a later date. She obviously knew she'd taken a step too far, knew her life was in danger." He folded one arm behind his head. "Why wouldn't it be from her? You and she are the only ones who know about the hiding place for the key, right?"

"I never told anyone, and as flakey as she was, I don't think Casey did, either, well, except Tony."

"Another reason is that Scott would have no need to send you a message like that. Why would he want to further pique your curiosity or provide you with any more evidence to bring to the authorities that Casey was anything more than a suicide?"

Martha had been panting, sipping in short

spurts of air. Filling her lungs, she closed her eyes. "I guess Casey really wanted me to talk to Tony."

"Do you think that's it?"

"What do you mean?" Martha asked.

"Maybe there's something more. Maybe this is what we've been waiting for, what Scott has been looking for."

"We looked in the cushion and found the key with the note. Are you saying there's something more?"

"It's a big, square cushion. You shoved your fingers into the zippered opening, found the key and the note. We didn't look for anything else. We didn't know there was anything else."

"The phone?"

"If we found that phone and it contained instructions from Scott, aka Ben, regarding Congressman Wentworth and the emails, we'd have some real proof against this guy. You wouldn't even have to admit to taking the emails. Your roommate died, you got this message from the grave and you found the phone. It all smelled like yesterday's fish, and you did your duty as a citizen and CIA employee and turned it over."

"You're making a lot of assumptions. Maybe she did just want me to contact Tony. It could be nothing more than that."

Cam flicked off the light and slid back beneath the covers. “Or a whole lot more.”

The following morning while they ate breakfast, Martha called Farah. When she ended the call, she picked up her fork and poked at the eggs on her plate. “She sounds fine, happy.”

“Was she suspicious that you were calling her?”

“A little. I don’t know if you heard, but I told her I wanted to check on her because she didn’t sound well last night.”

“As long as you didn’t spook her and didn’t spook Scott.” Cam rinsed off his plate and stacked it in the sink. “He’s keeping your silence today by holding on to Farah, but what about tomorrow and the days to follow?”

“Maybe he plans to leave the capital and isn’t worried even if I do report him. Is Farah ever going to believe Scott drugged and kidnapped her? As far as she’s concerned, he’s treating her to a spa day. What about your friend on the police force?”

“I called him this morning, but I can’t get the glass to him until tomorrow. I could just hold on to it and turn it over to the FBI once we report our suspicions about Farah’s boyfriend. And your father’s attorney? Have you called him?”

“While you were in the shower. He wants a

video conference with us later this afternoon." She held up her plate to him and he took it.

"Everything has to wait until we go back to your place and search that cushion for further evidence." He loaded the rest of their breakfast dishes from the sink into the dishwasher.

"You got a text." Martha held up his phone.

Cam dried his hands on a towel and hunched over the counter, holding out his hand for the phone. Martha dropped it in his palm and he opened the text.

"D-do you need any help reading it?"

He glanced up, a warm flush creeping up his neck to the roots of his hair. "Last night was just because of the stress of the situation. I'm okay."

"I'm sorry."

"Don't be. It's all right. I'm glad you asked." He held his phone under the light and read the text. "It's from one of my teammates, Joe. He's asking about my progress."

"Is he in the States?"

"Just arrived. He's taking leave for Christmas."

"What are you going to tell him?"

"The truth. That we're onto something and the emails were a setup, just as we suspected—not that we ever believed anything else."

"We'd better get going. If we find further

evidence in that seat cushion linking Scott to the murders, we'll have something more to discuss with Sam."

On the drive to Martha's town house, Cam texted back and forth with Joe. He wanted to warn him, just as Martha kept pointing out to him, that even if they could prove some foreign entity planted the emails implicating Denver, there was still the rest of the evidence against him. They wouldn't be able to clear his name right away, but this had to be a start.

The reporters had cleared out from the front of Martha's town house. Another Washington scandal had already diverted their attention, and Martha hadn't been around for days.

She pulled her car up to the curb. "I might as well collect my mail while I'm here and water some plants."

"First things first." Cam looked up and down the street. A few pedestrians walked to and from their cars. One with a dog waved to Martha and she waved back. Nobody looked suspicious, but then Scott was guarding his pampered captive.

Martha unlocked the front door, and Cam nudged her aside to walk in first. "Anything out of place?"

"Not this time, but I'm going to check Casey's room again." She bounded up the stairs ahead of him, and his heart pounded as he followed on her heels.

"Wait." He stopped her before she opened Casey's door. Holding his breath, he pushed it open.

The neat row of bags and the suitcase they'd packed up the other day greeted him, and he blew out a gust of air. "At least nobody's been back."

"I'm sure changing the locks helped." Martha placed her hands on her hips and surveyed the room. "Incredible I haven't even heard from Casey's mom yet."

"Do you know if they've made arrangements for her body?"

"I couldn't tell you." Martha wandered to the window and pressed her nose against the glass. "The patio furniture's still where we left it."

"Let's go take it apart."

They went downstairs and out the back door. Martha crouched beside the same chair.

"It wouldn't be in the other one?"

"We always used the same cushion for the key." She pulled the zipper back. This time she shoved her whole hand into the cover, wrinkling her nose. When most of her arm disappeared into the cushion, she squeaked. "I got it. Cam, it's a phone."

His pulse jumped. “It must be the phone she used for contact with Ben.”

Martha pulled out the type of phone typically sold as temp phones, and framed it in her hand. She pressed and held a button. “It’s dead.”

“Maybe she has a charger in her room. Did you see something?”

“I think just her regular smartphone charger.” She pressed the phone to her chest. “This is huge, Cam. This is what Scott was looking for, what he was afraid I’d find.”

“He must’ve thought Casey would have the phone on her when he lured her to that hotel room to kill her. When he couldn’t find it, he took her keys instead and searched her room for it.”

“It must have evidence pointing to him, or he wouldn’t have wanted it so badly.” A dog barked and Martha jumped.

Cam grabbed her arm. “Let’s go inside and find the charger. I cleaned out her desk and dumped a bunch of items in a plastic bag. It could be in there.”

Once inside, Cam took the stairs two at a time, clutching the phone in his fist. If the FBI could use the evidence on this phone to tie Scott to the murders and implicate him in the faked emails, Martha could completely avoid scrutiny for stealing the messages.

He pounced on the plastic bag containing the items from Casey's desk and dumped the contents onto the floor.

Martha dropped beside him and pawed through the papers, pens and business cards. She grabbed a black cord, pulled it free from the mess and dangled it from her fingers. "This could be it."

He grabbed the swinging end and compared it to the outlet on Casey's phone. "I think it is."

He inserted the USB into the phone and it clicked into place. "That's it."

Martha sprang to her feet in one movement. "Let's charge it downstairs. I take back every bad thing I said about Casey. Would a flake think to hide her cell phone where she knew I'd find it?"

"Not so fast. She's still a spy who stole secrets from a US congressman and worse…put her roommate's life in danger."

They traipsed down the stairs, and Martha pointed him to an outlet in the kitchen.

"Let's get this going. I can't wait to see what's on this phone."

Cam plugged the power cord into the outlet. "I suppose we can sit here and stare at it until it juices up."

The doorbell echoed through the house, and Martha gripped the edge of the counter. "Scott wouldn't be ringing my bell, would he?"

Cam pulled his gun from his jacket pocket and jerked his thumb at the door. "Check it out."

Martha crept to the door, crouching below the fan-shaped window at the top so the visitor couldn't see her coming. Cam stayed to the side, his gun at the ready.

She ducked her head and peered through the peephole. She whispered. "It's Sebastian."

"That guy you dated from work?" Cam rolled his eyes. "What does he want, a date? You don't have to answer the door."

"Martha? It's just Sebastian. I know you're home because I saw your car on the street. No press out here if you're worried."

Martha shrugged and slipped back the dead bolt. She opened the door wide enough so that Sebastian could see Cam hovering behind her.

He'd pocketed his weapon.

"This is a surprise."

"Is it?" Sebastian's eyes behind his glasses darted from Martha's face to Cam's. "I've been worried about you. First the congressman, then Casey and now the suspension from work."

"Speaking of work, why aren't you there?"

"I'm taking the whole week off for Thanksgiving. Aren't you going to visit your mother?"

"With all this going on—" she swept her arm behind her to encompass Cam "—I completely forgot about Thanksgiving."

Sebastian smiled and seemed to dig his Oxfords into the mat on Martha's porch. If Martha thought she was getting rid of this guy, she wasn't reading his signals.

"D-do you want to come in for a few minutes? We were just on our way out. I'm not staying here."

"At your mom's?" Sebastian stepped across the threshold, and a muscle ticked in Cam's jaw. This guy seemed to know a lot about Martha's family, but she *did* date him. Probably had a genius IQ.

Martha nodded toward Cam. "Sebastian, this is Cam. Cam, Sebastian."

Cam gave him a handshake that could've brought him to his knees if he'd kept it up, but he released his grip just as a grimace started to twist the other man's lips.

Sebastian put his hand behind his back. "Nice to meet you. Friend of Martha's?"

"Uh-huh." Cam wandered back to the charging phone and perched on the stool next to it while Martha and Sebastian talked.

She offered him a soda and he accepted. She couldn't be rude and kick the guy out?

As she walked toward the kitchen, her back to Sebastian, she rolled her eyes at Cam and pointed at the phone.

He shook his head.

She returned to Sebastian with a can in each hand and joined him on the sofa, where he'd made himself comfortable.

Cam ground his back teeth. Why was Sebastian here, anyway? Martha had made it clear they were over.

Cam kept one eye on the phone, and one ear on the conversation between Martha and Sebastian. He couldn't help it. Since his reading skills had been so poor in school, he'd honed his listening comprehension skills to an art.

Sebastian knew a lot about Martha's family, her father's situation, her mother's house. Her likes and dislikes. Their conversation had turned to art, and Cam felt a little bit of panic. Did he know enough about art to converse with Martha about it?

Martha said, "I'm not sure I know that artist."

"His work is similar to the print you have in your room."

"The Gaspar?"

Cam snorted softly. What the hell was a Gaspar?

Then something clicked in his brain, and his head twisted slowly to the side. Her room? The print in Martha's bedroom? Unless she'd been lying, Martha had told him she'd never slept with Sebastian, that he'd been to her place just twice and had never made it past the entryway.

How could he know what was in her bedroom—unless he'd seen it from her laptop camera, which he'd hacked into as the patriot?

Chapter Fifteen

Martha swallowed. "The Gaspar? In my bedroom?"

Sebastian licked his lips, his tongue flicking out of his mouth like a snake's. "The one you told me about."

Martha's eye twitched. Two seconds later, Cam barreled across the room and grabbed Sebastian by the neck.

Martha shouted, "What are you doing?"

"He's the patriot, Martha. He's the one who hacked your computer. He's the one who IDed you as the CIA employee to set up. He sent Scott to your mother's house, and Scott probably sent him here to watch your place while he's with Farah."

Martha's mouth dropped open, but every word Cam said she knew to be true. Sebastian had set her up, and he'd probably set up Farah, too.

Sebastian gagged and choked as his face

turned blue above Cam's powerful hand clutching his throat.

"Let him go, Cam. You're choking him."

He uncurled his fingers, and Sebastian slumped to the sofa, coughing.

Cam got in his face. "Start spilling."

Sebastian rubbed his throat. "You're crazy. I don't know what you're talking about."

"You can choose that route if you want." Cam pushed away from the sofa and held up the charging phone. "But we have Casey's burner phone. Is that what Scott sent you here to find?"

Sebastian dropped his head in his hands. "I—I didn't know it would go this far. It started with information. I was approached on an overseas trip. It was the money. They offered me so much money. You wouldn't know what it's like, Martha. You, with your privileged background. I had so much student loan debt, it was suffocating me."

"Oh, I thought you were doing it because you were such a *patriot*." Martha jumped up and took a turn around the room.

"How did this email plan start and why?" Cam slammed his fist in his palm. "Why Major Denver?"

Sebastian held up his hands as if deflecting physical blows. "I don't know anything about any of that. I was just asked to identify someone at Langley who would turn over a set of emails, no questions asked. I knew Martha would do it. I knew how she felt about her father's crimes."

"Oh my God. You used our conversations against me."

"It was nothing, Martha. You didn't have to be involved any more than turning over those emails—and then you broke bad."

"Ha!" She tossed her head. "That's quite a charge coming from someone involved in espionage against the government."

"It was more than just the emails. You helped Scott set up the liaison between Casey and Congressmen Wentworth, putting Martha in further danger."

"Martha was never supposed to be in danger."

"But she was." Cam smacked his hand against the wall, and Sebastian's eyes widened as his Adam's apple bobbed in his skinny neck.

How had she ever been remotely interested in him?

"I wanna know why Scott is still here. Why didn't he murder those people and get out of town?"

"I-I'm not sure."

Cam stalked toward him, and Sebastian

shrank against the sofa cushion. “I swear. I don’t know. Maybe it’s the phone. He wants to make sure we secure Casey’s phone first.”

His fist clenched, Cam loomed over Sebastian. “Who’s he with? Who is Scott working with?”

“I swear. I don’t know any of that.”

All three heads swiveled toward a buzzing noise from the phone.

“It’s operational.” Cam stepped away from Sebastian, flexing his fingers as if he’d gone through with the hit.

As Cam strode toward the counter, Sebastian half rose from the sofa, and Martha said, “Cam!”

He swung around and leveled a finger at Sebastian, who’d stopped in midrise. “Sit.”

Cam grabbed the phone and tapped it awake. “No password.”

“Check the texts.” Martha cast a nervous glance at Sebastian, who looked ready to bolt at any minute.

Cam’s eyebrows collided over his nose, and he thrust the phone out to Martha. “You look through it, while I watch our spy here.”

She took the phone from him.

Martha saw just two sets of texts, and one was the single text to her phone. The other was to a number, no name attached to it. It had to be the man Casey knew as Ben and they knew as Scott, but Martha would bet her town house that both names were false.

"The most recent text is the one directing Casey to the hotel for a meeting. She must've received that text, scheduled her text to me and then hid the phone in the hiding place for our key." Martha held up the phone. "This is enough to cast suspicion on Ben, even if this is a temp phone for him."

"Ben? Who the hell is Ben?" Sebastian shoved his glasses up the bridge of his nose.

Cam growled. "Ben is your buddy Scott. You know, the guy you set up with your coworker Farah. The guy who murdered three people."

"Ben?" Sebastian emitted a high-pitched, hysterical laugh. "He got that from when I told him I felt like a regular Benedict Arnold, and I had to explain who he was."

"He didn't know Benedict Arnold?"

"I don't think so."

"You were right about those emails, Martha. They came from a foreign entity, a nonnative speaker." Cam twirled his finger in the air. "What else? What other texts are between the two of them."

Martha backtracked through the conversation between Casey and Ben. "There's not a lot of substance here. It's mostly Ben setting up meetings. He must've been very careful about committing anything to text or probably even telephone conversations. I don't know why he was so worried about our finding this phone."

"Those texts are going to cast suspicion on Casey's death and Wentworth's. Maybe that's all we need."

Cam dragged a chair from the dining area, placed it in front of Sebastian and straddled it. "Here's what you're gonna do. We're gonna contact the FBI, and you're gonna confess to your crimes. You're gonna tell them about those faked emails and give them everything you know about Ben or Scott or whatever he calls himself. I have his fingerprints on a glass, and maybe we can get his real identity from his prints—even if it has to come from Interpol."

"We have to wait the rest of the day, Cam. He still has Farah, and if he finds out Sebastian went to the FBI, he could harm her."

"I—I can't stay here the rest of the day." Sebastian looked wildly from Martha to Cam. "I have plans for Thanksgiving."

Martha tapped Casey's phone against her chin. "What are we going to do with him? If we let him leave, he might disappear. If we call the FBI now, we put Farah in danger."

"If we let him leave, he just might go back to

the office and try to destroy the evidence that points to him as the one who got those emails to your computer."

"Wait. You can't keep me a prisoner." Sebastian shook his finger at Martha. "You're in a lot of trouble, Martha *Brockridge*."

"That makes two of us."

"We'll keep him here until Farah is safe. Maybe—" Cam drummed his fingers on the chair back "—we'll have him contact Ben and let him know he got Casey's phone."

"What? No!" Sebastian had turned even whiter. "He'd expect me to bring it to him right away."

"I still don't understand why tomorrow is some magic date for Ben. He releases Farah tomorrow, and we go through with our plans to report him once she's safe."

"He obviously plans to leave tomorrow."

"But why not leave today?"

Sebastian's eyebrows jumped to his hairline. "Why are you two looking at me? I told you. I don't know any of his plans. I'm paid for my contacts within the Agency and my access to and knowledge of its computers. That's it. When Wentworth died and then Casey, I knew everything had exploded."

Martha smoothed her thumb along the curve of Casey's phone. "If he's willing to give up

Farah tomorrow and take off, let him. I suppose he figures once he's out of the country, the FBI won't be able to track him down. But at least he'll be out of my life, and Sebastian can testify to the falsity of the emails."

"I won't know the why or who behind the setup of Major Denver though."

"Maybe once the FBI and CIA get a handle on Ben, it'll give them a good idea." She came up behind Cam and rubbed his shoulders. She couldn't help that Sebastian's bug eyes at the gesture gave her a thrill of satisfaction.

Casey's phone slipped from her hand and landed at Cam's foot. He bent forward to pick it up. "I'm not looking forward to spending the night with this guy, but... What's this?"

"What?" She leaned over his shoulder and looked at the phone cupped in his hand.

"Pictures. You didn't check the phone's photos, did you?"

"No." She knelt beside him, and even Sebastian hunched forward.

Cam's finger brushed across the display. "They're documents. Security plans and diagrams."

"For what?"

"I'm not sure yet. Casey must've gotten these from Wentworth. Tony told us she would get info from the congressman and pass it along to Ben. This must be part of that."

"Why would Ben want this type of information?"

"To gain knowledge of the security plans for a building or place…and bypass it."

Sebastian exhaled a noisy breath. "A terrorist attack. You'd want intel like that to plan a terrorist attack."

"He's right." Cam's lips formed a thin line. "And this is what Ben doesn't want us to see. He knows these pictures are on this phone."

When Cam swiped to the next picture, his body jolted. "It's the Mall, the monuments on the National Mall."

Martha crossed her arms over her chest. "And it's going down tomorrow."

Chapter Sixteen

"Answer it." Cam handed Sebastian his ringing phone, pressing the button on the side to activate the speaker.

They'd forced Sebastian to text Ben from Casey's phone to let him know he'd found it at Martha's town house. The response from Ben had been instantaneous.

Sebastian cleared his throat. "Scott."

"So you found it. How?"

"I—I remembered when I was dating Martha she told me Casey was always losing or forgetting her key, so they had a hiding place. I found the phone there."

"Did you look at anything on the phone?"

"Just the texts." Sebastian licked his lips. "Did you want me to look for something?"

"No, just bring it to me in two hours."

"Where are you?"

Cam dug his fingers into his biceps as they waited a beat for Ben's response.

"I took Farah to the St. Regis to get her out of the way while all this was happening. I didn't want her questioning Martha too closely about anything."

"Good idea."

"I don't need your approval, geek. Just bring me the phone."

Sebastian turned bright red. "Sure, sure. Am I supposed to see Farah while I'm there?"

"No need for that. We're ordering dinner up to our room tonight. I'll make an excuse to get ice or something, and you can meet me at the vending machines down the hall. Text me from the phone when you get here, so I know you still have it."

"Is this going to get me a bonus?" Sebastian wiped his upper lip with the back of his hand.

"Bonus?" Ben chuckled. "Sure, I'll give you a bonus."

When Sebastian ended the call, he gagged. "He's going to kill me."

Cam snatched the phone from his hand. "I'll try to save you…after I take care of Ben."

"And after I get Farah out of that room."

"Don't worry, Sebastian." Cam smacked him on the back. "This will all look better for you when you make your confession."

After a few informative hours at Martha's town house where Sebastian spilled his guts on video, Cam wiped Casey's phone clean and handed it to Sebastian.

"No tricks."

"Tricks? I don't have any tricks. I just want this to be over. I never imagined Ben would be planning a terrorist attack on our soil."

"So, it's okay on someone else's soil?" Martha yanked her coat from a hook by the door. "Your actions endangered so many lives."

"I didn't think."

"For a smart guy like you, that's quite an admission." Cam shoved his gun in his pocket. "Let's go."

With Sebastian in the back seat and Cam in the passenger seat beside her, Martha drove to the St. Regis near the Mall. "I guess he wanted to stay close to the site of his attack."

A valet took Martha's car, but they walked around to a side entrance. Their whole plan would blow up in their faces if Ben or Farah saw them in the lobby of the hotel.

They slipped through a side door and once inside, Cam prodded Sebastian in front of him until they reached an empty hallway leading to some restrooms. He slammed Casey's phone against Sebastian's chest. "Send the text."

He watched over Sebastian's shoulder as he texted the words, I'm here. Cam could read those words clear as day.

Less than a minute later, Ben called Sebastian on his own phone. Cam bent close to Sebastian's ear so he could hear the conversation.

"Where are you?"

"Lobby."

"I'm on the tenth floor. On one end of that floor, around the corner from the elevators, there's an alcove with vending and ice machines. Meet me there, hand over the phone and take your money. We're done."

"Will you be contacting me for further assignments?"

"We're done."

Ben ended the call.

Cam held out his hand. "I'll take that."

Sebastian dropped his phone into Cam's palm. "I just hope he doesn't call me again on my phone."

"Why would he?" He slipped Casey's phone into Sebastian's front pocket. "If you use that phone to double-cross me, I'll make sure I kill you both."

A bead of sweat ran down the side of Sebastian's face. "I'll follow the plan."

Cam turned to Martha. "As soon as I give you the signal from the stairwell, you text Farah and tell her to get out of that room as soon as she can. Once she's safe, call that number I gave you for the FBI. I'll surprise Ben in the vending room."

"Be careful." Martha grabbed his hand and pressed her lips against his cheekbone. "I may be losing you in a week, but I'm not going to lose you forever."

"I'm not gonna let that happen. Who's going to help me read my texts?" He kissed her mouth as Sebastian watched their exchange with round eyes.

"And you." He poked his finger in Sebastian's chest. "Give us a few minutes to climb ten flights of stairs before you even punch that elevator button."

"Got it."

They edged around the corner of the hallway and started to cross the lobby for the bank of elevators and the stairwell across from it. Their path took them past the crowded lobby bar.

"Martha?"

The voice sent a surge of adrenaline through Cam's veins, and he spun around. He made a grab for Martha's hand, but Farah had moved between them.

His gaze met Ben's above the women's heads, and his gut twisted.

Sebastian made a strange gulping sound beside him.

"Go, Martha!" His shout barely made it

above the music and conversation spilling out of the bar. He'd reacted too late, anyway.

Ben had Martha's arm and was pulling her back toward him.

Farah's dark eyebrows formed a V over her nose. "What's going on? What are you doing here? Sebastian? What are *you* doing here?"

Cam saw the flash of the blade in Ben's hand as he pressed it against Martha's side.

"Now I have a bigger prize." Ben smiled through his words as if they were all part of the convivial bar scene behind them.

"I—I don't understand." Farah's head was snapping back and forth between Ben and Martha, and Cam and Sebastian.

Cam took Farah's hand and pulled her toward him. "You're safe now."

"Safe?" Farah sobbed and stretched her hand out. "Martha?"

Martha drew back her shoulders and straightened her spine, standing taller than the man who held her at knifepoint. "The man you know as Scott is planning a terrorist attack."

"No, I..."

"Shh." Ben put his finger to his lips. "Quiet, Farah, unless you want to see your friend hurt. I at least had some feelings for you. Her? I don't care about her at all."

Farah's shoulders slumped and she dropped her head.

Cam pulled Farah behind him. "What are you going to do with Martha?"

"Just like Farah, Martha stays with me until I can conduct my business tomorrow."

Cam ground his words through his teeth. "Your business is terror, mayhem, murder of innocents."

"So is yours, Sergeant Sutton."

A lash of heat whipped through Cam's body, and he curled his fists. "You'll have to kill all of us to carry out your plan. We all know."

"I think I just need Martha. Do you want to see her die right here and now to save a bunch of strangers on the Mall tomorrow? And how do you know I don't have others to take my place?"

"Oh, we'll be prepared for you and others like you. Planning a truck or van attack, aren't you? Planning to mow down some civilians? Once I outline your plans to the FBI and DC Metro Police, they'll be ready for you."

That got him.

Ben's eyes, which had been focused on Cam the entire time, widened, and his arm slipped an inch from Martha's waist.

Cam would have to act here and now in the

hotel lobby. He'd never allow this man to take Martha away from him—not now, not ever.

A muscle in his jaw twitched as he sensed movement behind him from Sebastian, who'd remained speechless and frozen up until this point.

Sebastian took a deep breath and shouted. "Help! Help!"

Ben's head jerked up, and Martha wrenched away from him, creating just enough space for Cam to make a move.

Cam lunged forward and grabbed the wrist of the hand that held the knife, and twisted. A woman in the bar screamed.

Ben made a thrusting motion to the side, and Cam slammed his body against Ben's, knocking him over, his hand still grappling for the knife.

They landed with a thud, and people began shouting around them. Hands grabbed at the back of Cam's jacket as moisture began seeping into the front of his shirt.

Ben released the knife, and Cam found himself in sole possession of it. He pushed himself off Ben, and the wound beneath Ben's heart began gushing blood.

"Cam?" Martha dropped to the floor, her hand on the back of his neck.

"I'm fine. It's not me." Cam looked into the

dying man's eyes and grabbed the front of his shirt. "Not yet, you bastard. Who sent you? Why'd you set up Denver?"

A trickle of blood seeped from Ben's mouth as his lips curled into a smile.

Epilogue

Martha stretched out on the huge bed in the penthouse suite of the St. Regis and curled her toes. “It’s a shame we have this big bed and end up crowding together in one corner of it every night.”

“A shame?” Cam grabbed her foot and kissed her arch. “We can just crowd together on another corner of the bed if you want to make good use of it.”

She sat up and wrapped her arms around Cam, burying her head against his chest. “Promise me you’ll come back to me safe and sound after this deployment.”

“That’s the easy part.” He ran his knuckles down her spine. “Promise me you won’t engage in any more illegal activities.”

“I’m done breaking bad, as Sebastian put it, although he’s the one who’s going to be spending time in federal prison.”

"His actions after we confronted him went a long way toward reducing his sentence."

"And his sheer cowardice when he screamed and started scrambling for his own safety allowed you to take down Ben." Martha suppressed a shiver. "I can't believe we wound up uncovering a terrorist attack. He had the van already rented and everything. There would've been plenty of people on the Mall the day before Thanksgiving."

Cam's muscles tensed beneath her touch. "He died before I could get any answers out of him, although we know he killed Tony and Casey and made sure Casey got together with Wentworth to get info from him about Denver."

"He must've killed Wentworth too after Casey got the info about Denver out of him, even though the authorities are still calling Wentworth's death a heart attack. Maybe they'll take a second look at that now that Interpol identified him as Alain Dumont, a Frenchman of Algerian descent, a man involved in petty crimes but with no known terrorist ties…but we know he's not working alone."

She rubbed his back. "His involvement with the emails is forcing the CIA to take a closer look at the evidence against Major Denver."

"A closer look is not clearing him."

"I know. I'm sorry." She flattened her hands against his chest and pushed away from him. "If you say he's innocent, I believe you and others will, too."

"Even Asher, one of our own teammates..." He shook his head. "I don't want to get into all that when we have just a few days left together. How's Farah holding up?"

"She's fine. Feels humiliated, but maybe this whole thing cured her of her propensity for unavailable men."

"No way she's going to top that guy for unavailability." Cam ran his hand up her thigh. "And you? Looks like you wound up with someone unavailable yourself."

"I'm willing to wait."

"Good, because I fell in love with the smartest girl in class, and I'm not about to let her slip through my hands." He scooped her into his lap and tore off her robe.

"Oh, I like where this is going, D-Boy." She reached for her glasses, and he grabbed her hand.

"Nope, I wanna make love to you wearing nothing but your glasses."

And then he did and the sparks flew.

* * * * *

Look for the next book in
award-winning author Carol Ericson's new
Red, White and Built: Pumped Up miniseries,
Delta Force Daddy, *available next month.*

And don't miss the titles in her
Red, White and Built miniseries,
which introduced us to some sexy,
powerful Navy SEALs:

Locked, Loaded and SEALed
Alpha Bravo SEAL
Bullseye: SEAL
Point Blank SEAL
Secured by the SEAL
Bulletproof SEAL

Available now from Harlequin Intrigue!